MARY PLAIN IN TOWN

GWYNEDD RAE

with Illustrations by
IRENE WILLIAMSON

ROUTLEDGE & KEGAN PAUL LTD.
LONDON AND BOSTON

First published in 1935
by Routledge & Kegan Paul Ltd
Broadway House, 68-74 Carter Lane
London, EC4V 5EL
and 9 Park Street, Boston, Mass. 02108 U.S.A.
Reprinted 1936, 1938, 1941, 1942 (twice), 1943 (twice),
1944, 1947, 1949, 1951, 1956, 1962, 1972 and 1973
Printed in Great Britain by
Redwood Press Limited
Trowbridge, Wiltshire

ISBN 0 7100 1989 0

This book is for
Mary's great friend,
MARK

CONTENTS

CHAPTER   PAGE

INTRODUCTION — vii

I   MARY GIVES AN ENGLISH LESSON — 9

II   MARY IS TAKEN ILL AND FRISKA IS TAKEN IN — 16

III   MARY BETS A BET — 25

IV   IN WHICH A BET LEADS TO A SVISIT — 31

V   MARY WINS AGAIN — 38

VI   WHICH IS VERY MARY — 45

VII   ABOUT TWINS AND TELEPHONES AND A SHIPWRECK — 52

VIII   MARY SVISITS A DANCING-CLASS — 61

IX   MARY GOES TO SCHOOL — 70

X   WHICH HAS GOT MARY, MEASLES AND MURPHY IN IT — 79

XI   THE FIRE THAT WASN'T — 86

XII   MARY GOES TO THE CINEMA — 94

XIII   IN WHICH MARY GOES JUBILEEING — 102

XIV   MARY GOES TO THE B.B.C. — 110

INTRODUCTION

To children who may meet Mary Plain for the first time in this book I must explain that she is a real bear, who was born in the bear-pits at Berne. But she is also a very special kind of bear so, of course, she has very special adventures and these are some more of them. In the other two books, *Mostly Mary* and *All Mary*, you can read all about Mary Plain's early life in the pits at Berne and of how she came, on what she called a 'svisit,' to England with the Owl Man and won a first prize at a Show. I am afraid there is no doubt that the Show turned Mary's head a little but I do hope that her friends will not like her any the less for it.

GWYNEDD RAE

THE BEAR FAMILY TREE

ALPHA and LADY GRIZZLE'S FAMILY

BIG WOOL   *grandmother to* MARY.

BIG WOOL'S FAMILY

YOUNG WOOL (*dead*)   *father to* MARY.

FRISKA   *aunt to* MARY.

BUNCH   *uncle to* MARY.

FORGET-ME-NOT ⎫   *aunts to* MARY, *but younger than*
PLUM   ⎭   *she.*

FRISKA'S FAMILY

MARIONETTA ⎫   *cousins to* MARY.
LITTLE WOOL ⎭

HARRODS. *A cross bear with no relations.*

AND

MARY (*called* PLAIN). *An orphan.*

CHAPTER ONE

MARY GIVES AN ENGLISH LESSON

" Now, now, now ! " said Friska, bringing her stick sharply down on the edge of the stone bath. " Little Wool ! Will you please attend to me ? Marionetta ! "

The twins' heads came round to face their mother but their eyes stayed sideways on Mary who was in a corner of Nursery Pit, apparently in paroxysms of laughter. It was a good thing she had her back turned because anyone, with half a glance at Mary's face, could see it wasn't amused. Neither was the laugh amused really, but then Mary wasn't laughing because she was amused but because she wanted to annoy Friska. And she did. If she could only have known how Friska's paws itched to box her ears !

The same scene happened every morning. It had happened every day since Mary, fresh from her svisit to England, had refused to attend lessons unless they were given in English.

Friska had been very fussed and upset. " But Mary," she

expostulated, "English is all very well when you are in English but—"

"England," corrected Mary.

"England," repeated Friska before she could stop herself. How dared Mary correct her !

"But," she went on, her voice trembling a little, "you must not on any account forget your Switzerland."

"Swiss," corrected Mary.

"Swiss," said Friska, again before she could stop herself and then, drawing herself up so as to be as much taller than Mary as she possibly could, she said, in her growliest voice, "I wish to goodness you had stopped in Engzerland ! "

Poor Friska, she was in a very difficult position. She could, of course, appeal to Big Wool, the cubs' grandmother, and Big Wool would instantly put her paw down and Friska knew, all the bears knew, what a firm paw Big Wool had. But that meant acknowledging that she, Friska, couldn't manage her own niece and a small niece at that and this she could not bring herself to do. So Mary went on being disturbing in the corner, and Friska's paws went on itching to box her ears and the twins went on being inattentive on the edge of the bath until one morning Friska couldn't bear it any longer and, swallowing her pride, a big lump of it, she resolved to approach Mary once more.

She always came over into Nursery Pit for half an hour every morning to give the cubs their lessons before she herself was shut into Parlour Pit for the day. So one day she said on her arrival, " There will be no class this morning, cubs, because I want to have a little chat with Mary."

The twins chased each other up the tree with whoops of

delight, while Mary followed Friska into the corner, wondering very much what the little chat would be about.

Friska cleared her throat. " Mary," she began, " first of all I would like you clearly to understand that the only reason I do not know any English is because I have never had any time to learn it." Here she stopped a minute just to wish that it had been French that Mary was making all the fuss about, for Friska knew quite a lot of French. She knew that ' oui ' meant ' little ' for instance, and that ' carotte ' meant ' carrot ' and that when someone said ' Bonjour ' the answer was ' Encore.' " Now I feel it is a great pity that you should be missing all these lessons and one day you'll be sorry. Nobody wants to grow up stupid, do they ? "

" Don't they ? " asked Mary.

Friska hastily tucked her right paw behind her back. " No," she growled, " and what's more—you know it."

" But then I'm not stupid," said Mary. " How could I be, when I'm an unusual first-class bear with a white rosette and a gold medal with a picture of myself and a—"

" Yes, yes," interrupted Friska, impatiently, " but what I wanted to tell you was that I am not quite so busy just now and if you—well, if you would like to -er- well—talk to me in English, I will, of course, learn it very quickly. And then," she finished brightly, " we could all do our lessons together again."

" Certainly, Auntie," said Mary sweetly. " And what would you like me to teach you first ? "

Friska tucked her second paw away.

" Please," she said, " recite my poem about St. Bruin's

Day." Mary might have been to England but at least she hadn't written a poem.

Now Mary only knew two sentences in English. One was 'English spoken' which she had learnt from the door of a barber's shop, but she was awfully good at inventing. "Very well," she said, "will you please step into the schoolroom?" and she pointed to the bath. Friska retreated a little further into the corner. She had not bargained for this.

"Oh no, Mary," she said, "I–er–I think it would be more— well—fitting to stay quietly here in the corner. No one will notice us here." Which was a silly thing to say to Mary who, above all things, liked being noticed.

"Just as you like," said Mary, "but no schoolroom, no English," and she walked away with her head in the air.

When she had walked as far as she could without running into the wall she turned and saw that Friska was already sitting on the extreme edge of the bath—right up at the end which was the top of the class. Friska hoped Mary wouldn't notice this. "Ha—Ha!" thought Mary to herself, noticing at once. She strolled back towards the bath and said, quite kindly, "Shall we begin now?"

Friska nodded. She was beyond words.

"Manyery happery yearsery we-pop wishery to-pop youery," said Mary, very fast indeed. Friska blinked.

"Are you quite sure that's right, Mary?" she asked. "It sounds very odd to me."

Mary raised her eyebrows and tapped impatiently on the floor with her paw, exactly like Friska did when the cubs were slow at their lessons.

"Of course it's right," she said. "Do you think I could

make a mistake ? Wasn't I five whole days in England ?
Aren't I an unusual first-class bear with a white ro—"

"Yes, yes," said Friska, who was sick of Mary's list and
bothered if she was going to listen to it twice in one day.

"Very well then, go on," said Mary, a bit sulky because she
hated her list being interrupted.

Friska swallowed.

"Many – happy – er – pop – years we – wish –to – pop –
you," she said, "oh, and ery."

Mary pointed with her stick.   "Kindly move to the bottom
of the class," she said.   Friska moved, with a nervous look up
at the railings to see if anyone was watching her disgrace.
There, by rights, she should have stayed but Mary enjoyed
moving her up and down and if her English didn't progress,
her body did, from one end of the seat to the other, till where
she sat got quite hot and sore from all the sliding.   At the end
of the time she was so muddled and out of breath that she
actually bargained with Mary.

"If you will come to lessons and do your very best to be
good," she said, "once a week I will allow you to give the
twins an English lesson."

"You, too," said Mary quickly.

"I said the twins," said Friska.

"Then, no," said Mary, starting to walk away.

"Very well, me too," said her aunt, who knew when she
was beaten.

So that night Friska went to bed feeling rather nervous but
hoping for the best and Mary went to bed, very chirpy, but
hoping, hard, for the worst.

And if you should happen to pass the pits on a Wednesday

morning you will see the three cubs sitting sedately along the
edge of the bath and you will hear them chanting the bears'
multiplication table :—

> 2 *smiles make* 1 *laugh.*
> 4 *sneezes make* 1 *cold.*
> 2 *much racing makes* 1 *tired.*
> 10 *licks make* 1 *clean.*
> 20 *carrots make* 1 *full.*

But on Saturdays, if you should happen that way, you will
see a very different sight.   The two cubs will be wriggling so
hard that every minute you will wonder how soon they will
fall backwards into the bath, and beyond them, still at the

bottom of the class and still on the very edge of the bath, you will see Friska, still with an anxious eye on the railings above, while before them, brandishing her stick, her legs very wide apart, stands Mary.

" Now then ! " she shouts, as if they were all deaf.   " All together ! "

" God save the King."

Which was the rest of the English that Mary knew.

CHAPTER TWO

ONE morning when Friska called the cubs to their lessons, Little Wool came running out of their sleeping-den and said, " Mary can't come, she's ill.   She can't stand up and she's very ill indeed."

While Little Wool was telling Friska this sad news, Mary, curled up on her bed of straw, was having a private laugh. The truth of the matter was that, ever since her visit to England, Mary had been a bit too big for her boots and wanted all the attention for herself.   Now that the baby aunts, Forget-me-not and Plum, were bigger, they were let out into Nursery Pit on fine days from eleven o'clock until three o'clock, and all the people of Berne leant over the stone wall and cried, " Aren't the baby ones sweet ! " which annoyed Mary exceedingly.

So one day, she determined to be ill, because ill people just have to be noticed.   " They'll be sorry when I'm gone to bed," she thought to herself.

" Yes," said Little Wool again, " she's very ill."

" Tut, tut," said Friska as she bustled off to visit her suffering niece.

Mary, indeed, seemed to be far from well, judging from the groans she was giving ; every time they lifted her up, her knees seemed to fold up and down she went again.

" Put your tongue out, please," said Friska.

Mary obeyed gladly, shooting it out as far as it would go.

" It seems a little long," said Friska, uncertainly.   Then, " Whereabouts are you ill, Mary dear ? " she asked, hoiking her to her feet.

" All over," said Mary, folding up again.

Friska, thoroughly alarmed, sent for Big Wool, who arrived, looking very capable.   Friska rushed up to her excitedly.   " Mary's very ill," she said.   " She's ill in her legs and in her front and in her back and in her head—"

" Ssh ! " said Big Wool sternly, who considered Friska had lost her own head.   Friska sshushed at once.   " Leave her to me," she went on, starting to hoik, " I'll manage her.   Now then, Mary, upsy daisy ! "

But there was no upsy and very little daisy about Mary just then, who continued to fold up and to moan till Job, their keeper, arrived to send them all to their own pits for the day. Big Wool stepped forward and explained about Mary, and Job, giving her a quick glance, said to Friska, " You'd better stay with her—I'll give you something for her," as he hustled the other bears away.

Presently he returned with a hot sandbag, a bowl of water, two dry biscuits and a bandage.   " You can tie it on with this," he said as he went off.   " Very well," said Friska, not at all sure what she had to tie on to where.   While she was wondering about it, Mary, who had had no breakfast and who had

"I don't really think you need tell me how to manage a bandage"

stopped folding up, wasted no time in wondering what to do with the biscuits.

Friska, meantime, carefully unrolled the bandage and then, picking up the sandbag, she popped it on to Mary's head and said bracingly, " We'll soon have you better, Mary dear ! " She always called people who were ill ' dear.'   " Just hold this against your head," and she handed Mary one end of the bandage and then set out to find the other end herself.   When she had found it she was a good way off from Mary.

" Do you know how ? " asked Mary, suspiciously.

" Really, Mary dear," said Friska, " I don't think, no I don't *really* think, you need tell me how to mandage a bandage ! " She began walking slowly round Mary and every time a loop went round Mary's head a corresponding loop went round Friska's waist till, at the end, they were so closely looped that, if it hadn't been for the bag on Mary's head, you couldn't have told which was which.

By this time, the heat had penetrated Mary's fur and was causing her great discomfort.

" It's burning me, my head's on fire, take it off ! " she shrieked.

" There, there," said Friska, who knew for a certainty that unless someone let them out they were both in the bandage for good.   " Be a good girl, there's a dear."

" I'm not a dear and oh, I wish I wasn't here," shouted Mary. " Take it off, I say."

" There, there," said Friska again just because she could think of nothing else to say.

But Mary, maddened at being burned and there-there'd, wriggled desperately to get free, and catching her foot in a loop of bandage brought them both to the floor, winding Friska completely. For a moment she lay making kind of dying noises, while Mary, not caring in the least if she died twice, went on being burned and trying to get loose. Then, having got her breath back, Friska, seeing the bowl of water close at hand, poured it over Mary's head. " There, Mary dear," she said. And it must be confessed the ' dear ' was nearly a spit !

At this moment the door opened and Job appeared. He stood and gazed at them with his mouth open. Friska lay on her back with Mary's head still attached affectionately to her front, the sandbag at a rakish angle over one eye. She was furious with Mary. Furious with her for being ill, furious with her for tripping her up, and furious with her for being so close.

" What's she listening to ? " asked Job, much interested. " Listening to what you had for breakfast ? "

"She's not listening to anything," said Friska with as much dignity as she could assume under the circumstances, and Mary. " It's—well—I tied it on—but we're tied too."

Job whipped out his knife, bent down, and in a moment they were freed. Friska got up, feeling her damp front and glaring at Mary. Mary started to glare back but Job soon put an end to that by producing an ugly-looking black bottle and a spoon.

" Open your mouth, Mary," he said. Mary took one sniff.

" Oh, but I'm quite well now, thank you," she said. " Extra well."

" I daresay, but we'll be making sure of it," said Job and gripping Mary between his knees, he seized her by the nose so that she had to open her mouth to breathe and poured a large spoon of warm castor-oil down her throat.

Which is what always happens to bears that pretend.

A day or two after this, Mary was sitting on the bath and thinking of how dull everything seemed to be, when suddenly she heard a voice say, " Hallo, Mary Plain ! "   Looking up, she saw her great friend, the Owl Man.   She hurried up the tree and out along a branch.   She always did this when he came so as to get as close to him as possible.

" You're not looking very gay this morning," said the Owl Man.

" No," said Mary, " I'm feeling un-gay."

" Everything rather dull, not much fun, eh ? " enquired the Owl Man.   Mary nodded.

" I thought so," he said.   " I know exactly what's wrong with you, Miss Plain.   You're suffering from swollen head. It's a nasty complaint."

Mary felt her head carefully all over.   " Whereabouts ? " she said.   " I can't see where."

" No, but everyone else can," said the Owl Man with a laugh.   " Now, there's only one cure for that and that is, get busy."

" Busy over what ? " asked Mary.

The Owl Man thought a moment and then he said, "How about those young aunts of yours ?   Couldn't you give them swimming or drill or lessons or something ? "

Mary brightened.   She definitely didn't like the aunts enough to play with them, but she did like them enough to teach them.

" I'll try," she said.

"That's right," said the Owl Man. "It shall be a surprise—a goodbye surprise for next Tuesday."

"Goodbye, did you say?" asked Mary edging a little nearer along the branch.

"Yes, I'm off to England next day," said the Owl Man.

"Didn't you want a svisitor this time then?" asked Mary hopefully.

"I'm afraid not, old girl," said the Owl Man. "Some day, perhaps. Now, you get busy over that surprise."

So Mary worked hard all that week and when the Owl Man turned up on Tuesday she paraded the aunts in front of him.

"Now, both together! One, two, three!" And the aunts sang in high squeaky voices (to the tune of *Polly put the kettle on*):—

Forget-me-not :   " Once there was a clever bear
Plum   clever bear
                              clever bear "

Forget-me-not :   " Once there was a clever bear
Both together :   a clever bear."

Chorus. *Forget-me-not :*   " Now you try and guess her name
   Plum :   guess her name
               guess her name "
   Forget-me-not :   " Now you try and guess her name
   Both :   and guess her name."

The remainder of the song was sung as above.

     " And she once went s'visiting
         s'visiting
         s'visiting "
     " And she once went s'visiting
       This clever bear."

    " Now you try and guess her name
        guess her name
        guess her name "
    " Now you try and guess her name
      and guess her name."

    " And she won a white rosette
       white rosette
       white rosette "
    " And she won a white rosette
      This first class bear."

    " Now you try and guess her name
        guess her name
        guess her name "
    " Now you try and guess her name
      It's MARY PLAIN."

" Oh Mary," said the Owl Man, wiping his eyes, " I might have known I could bank on you,"

" How do you mean—bank ? " asked Mary.

" I mean bank on it's being a real Mary surprise," said the Owl Man.

" Was it very Mary then ? " asked Mary.

" Exceedingly," said the Owl Man.

CHAPTER THREE

MARY BETS A BET

RATTLE, bang ! Down came the door of Lady Grizzle and Alpha's sleeping-den.

Bubble, bubble, bubble, went Mary.

Rattle, bang ! This time it was Big Wool and her family who were locked behind their iron doors. Rattle, bang ! And now the twins were safe for the night.

Bubble, bubble, oh thank goodness, bubble, went Mary.

Job sighed as the last door went rattling home. He was always glad to get them safely shut up for the night. Bears could give a lot of trouble and often did, especially since that Mary Plain had got back from England. The way she bossed those young cubs, Forget-me-not and Plum, teaching them to salute her and God saving the King. It was a wonder the other bears put up with her sometimes and yet, come to think of it, Mary Plain was the kind of bear one did put up with, whatever she did. He smiled as he let down the last door. Well, she was safe for to-night, anyway.

But she wasn't.

Bubble, bubble, oh do go, bubble, before I burst, went Mary, as Job went off home.

For a moment the little black disc with the two holes in it went on floating quietly on top of the water in the bath but presently, with an extra big bubble, it came popping up and turned into Mary's nose and behind it came the rest of Mary, very damp indeed. She climbed out of the bath and shook herself.

That morning she had bet a bet with herself. " Mary Plain, I bet you won't be able to hide and stay out in the pit all night, so there ! " And now she had won the bet and it didn't seem to matter very much. All that mattered was that she was extremely cold and wet. She climbed up the tree and sat on a branch where a moonbeam was shining. She had never been out at night before and thought what a pale sun it was, as she waited for it to dry her. But it didn't. Ten minutes later she was just as shivery and cold so she thought she'd better go to bed with the others after all. Also, she thought she would give up betting in future.

Climbing down, she went and stood outside the den where the twins slept with the baby aunts. How they would get her in she didn't stop to think, but she was sure they could if they tried. About a foot from the ground holes were pierced through the iron to let in some air, so Mary put her mouth against one of these and said, " Twins ! I'm tired of betting and I want to come in. I don't like it out here."

" Rrrrch, rrrrch," snored the twins.

" Aunts ! " tried Mary next. " Forget-me-not, do please let me in. Aunt Plum ! "

But Forget-me-not and Plum only answered " Rrrrch, rrrrch."

So she moved on to the next den door where Friska and Big Wool and the others slept and, standing outside, with little runnels of water running down her front and little shivers of cold running down her back, she tried again.

" Auntie ! It's me ! I fell in the bath and I'm wet." Pause. " I'm sorry for last time I was naughty." Pause. " And for all the times before. Do please let me in." Pause .nd then, very persuasively, " Nice, *clever* Friska." But the only answer she got was " Erruch zi bu, erruch zi bu," from Friska, who prided herself on snoring with a French accent.

Before the third and last door Mary's legs trembled a little and not only from cold. She gave a little bow and then said, " Sir, I'm the cub, sir, what gave you the little whistle you liked, sir, and I'm wet, sir. Could I come in, sir, please ? I wouldn't take much room, sir." But the terrifyingly growly snores that came out sent Mary hurrying away.

Suddenly she caught sight of an unfamiliar lump in a corner of the pit—a big lump it was. Hurrying across she saw with delight that it was a bundle of soiled straw, tied together in the middle, which had been turned out of the sleeping dens when the fresh straw had been put in that evening. Just exactly what she most wanted. She climbed in, burrowing deep into the straw till it closed about her—a warm tickly nest. " I'm glad I betted, after all," she said and dropped off to sleep.

Because Mary was very tired she slept a long sleep and when she woke up she couldn't, for a moment, remember where she was. Then a piece of straw tickled her on the nose and she remembered. Of course she had betted herself into the bath and then into the straw. But what a funny thing, the straw seemed to be moving! At least not so much moving as kind of trembling all round Mary. Very carefully, she poked her head out and found, to her amazement, that instead of one fir tree fixed in the middle of the pit, there were lots of them, all moving up to her and then moving out of sight beyond the straw.

Now Mary thought she knew a lot, but she had to confess she hadn't an idea, not a single idea, that trees could walk. " This is what comes from betting! " she told herself, as she pushed her head a little further out.

Then she understood. It wasn't the trees that were moving but she, herself, and the straw, because she and the straw were both in a cart. Listening carefully, she heard voices, a deep slow one and then a quicker one, answering. So she wasn't alone and Mary was glad about this for, devoted as she was to Mary Plain (and really there wasn't any one else she knew of that she was quite so fond of), she didn't awfully like being all alone with her—not for long. But, as Mary stared out of the straw, with one tufty bit sticking very becomingly behind her ear and saw the two backs that belonged to the voices, she knew one thing for certain. The two backs didn't know she was there or they wouldn't stay backs but would turn quickly into faces, which was what always happened when Mary was about. So she got under the straw again till she could settle what to do, and while she was settling, dropped off to sleep again.

She was awakened by a violent lurch and the next moment she was sliding downwards with the straw. First she was upside down and then she was downside up and then there was a bump and a bang and a noise of wheels rattling away.

Mary fought her way out of the straw and came out looking very ruffled and untidy with bits of it sticking all over her coat. She was standing at what seemed to be the end of a road with a wood behind her.   Mary didn't much like being at the end of anything so she decided she'd rather go with the wheels.

" Hi ! " she shouted, but the wheels went on rattling away and though she ran to the corner and shouted " Hi ! " again, they were far out of sight, so Mary gave it up and came back to the straw again.   She came back to the straw because it was the only thing she knew and just then she wanted rather badly to be near something she knew.   She'd never been out alone before and she wasn't sure about roads that ended.   She sat down on the straw, feeling extra small, and for Mary to feel extra small meant she was in a very bad way.   To cheer herself up she started talking to herself.

" Now, Mary Plain," she said, holding her left paw tightly with her right, " let's hold paws for company and talk a bit, shall we ? "

" Yes," said Mary Plain.

" How are you feeling ? " asked Mary.

" Terribly hungry," groaned Mary Plain.   Mary knew only too well how true this was, so she hastily changed the subject.

" I like straw," she said conversationally.

" Yes," said Mary Plain again.

" I like the smell," said Mary, very much hoping that Mary Plain would find something more interesting to say this time but she didn't, she just said " Yes " again.

Now, Mary's inside was feeling so like a big empty hole that she took some deep breaths of air to fill it up a bit and the air she breathed smelt of straw and the smell of the straw was a smell of things you know very well, a homey smell—a beary smell.

" Oh," said Mary, feeling smaller than ever, " do you think the twins are happy without me ? "

But no one answered.   Not even Mary Plain.

CHAPTER FOUR

IN WHICH A BET LEADS TO A SVISIT

'Now, that's the very last time you bet, Mary Plain, and don't forget!" said Mary, as she got up off the pile of straw. She turned and looked at the wood. It was rather dark with a little green path under the trees which seemed to say "Follow me!" But Mary wasn't sure about woods either, and especially alone. She looked round to see if she could see anyone about, but there was still only the end of the road and the straw, so, facing the wood again, she squared her shoulders and, cocking her head on one side, said, "Mary Plain, I bet you you won't go into that wood," and marched off under the trees.

For a long time the path went on saying "Follow me" and Mary followed and then suddenly she saw, lying at her feet, what looked like a brown saucer upside down. Now, saucers usually mean food and Mary was terribly wanting food so she bent and picked it up and then she got the fright of her life. For out from under the saucer popped a tiny and very angry head. "How dare you impede my progress!" it said. "Replace me instantly. Instantly, fur-covered busy-body!"

Mary obeyed so promptly that the saucer reached the ground rather too quickly for comfort and this and the fact that it was also upside down, made it angrier still.

31

" Restore my equilibrium, you officious perambulating hay-stack ! " it spluttered furiously.

Mary wasn't at all partial to being called a hay-stack, or any of the other things for the matter of that, but she had never seen anything so small so angry before, so she turned it carefully the right side up and then said, politely, " What are you ? I'm Mary Plain." And she gave a little bow.

" Anyone can see that," said the saucer rudely. " *What* am I, indeed ! I presume you mean 'Who' ! Unmannerly pickthank ! "

" Who, sir," said Mary, still willing to oblige because of its angriness and because of its being right in the middle of the path so she couldn't pass. " I thought perhaps you were called 'Mr Saucer' ? "

But at this the saucer went off into such a series of explosions that Mary backed away.

" I'll teach you to make puns about my shape," it said, rising on its hind legs and advancing on Mary threateningly, " you bearded baggage ! "

Mary, in retreat, suddenly couldn't bear to be called a single name more, so she said " Good-afternight," not quite sure, owing to the darkness of the wood, if it was day or night and, taking her courage in her paw, she gave a flying leap for safety.

" Grasshopper ! " she heard it spit, as she passed the danger zone and then " Capering kangaroo ! "

But Mary, safely out of range, ran as fast as she could till, arriving at the end of the wood, she found herself in broad sunshine on the edge of a big green field with more trees beyond. In the middle of the field stood a red cow and beside it a bucket and stool. Mary trotted up to it, hoping very

After that there was a long silence

much it would be a friendly cow.   It swung its head slowly round and looked at her.

" Moo," it said.

" Moo," said Mary back, determined not to offend.

" Moo, moo," said the cow, and " Moo, moo, moo," said Mary, going one better.

" Moo ? " said the cow enquiringly, but Mary felt she simply couldn't go on saying ' moo ' so, only too pleased, as always, to introduce herself, she said, " I'm Mary Plain, an unusual first-class bear with a white ro— Oh dear ! " she broke off, suddenly catching sight of the bucket, " I'm so empty."

After that there was a long silence and after the silence Mary was a completely different shape.

She sat down on the grass for a bit but, almost at once, she was alarmed by the sound of loud shouts and, turning round, she saw racing towards her two boys and a man, holding a rope in his hand.

Now Mary had been lassoed once before, and at sight of that rope she made off across the field towards the trees.   Wisely choosing a pine which had no branches near the bottom, she swarmed up it and a moment later was safely at the top.

The two boys tried to climb up the slippery trunk with no success while Mary, quite safe and quite full and therefore quite happy, sat astride a branch and pelted them with fir-cones from above.   " Baggage ! " she shouted, " Hopperoo ! " enjoying herself mightily and maddening the boys.

In the end their father, saying he'd stay and keep a watch on her himself, sent them off home and, settling himself at the foot of the tree, he lighted his pipe.   Mary, remembering the rude saucer had called her a hay-stack, began picking off some of the

bits of straw sticking to her.   That done, she began to look
about for something else to do.   But there isn't much you can
do on the top of a pine-tree, so presently she climbed down a
little way and was rewarded by the comforting sound of a
snore.   So he was asleep !   " Hurrah," thought Mary, " I'm
off ! "   But she determined to run no risks—not with ropes
about.   So she crept down a bit further and out along a
branch and, leaning over, gripped the branch below and
began pulling her own down to meet it.   Whether she pulled
too hard, we shall never know but, the next instant, Mary was
performing the most wonderful acrobatic feat of her life.   For
the under branch cracked and the upper one, released, sprang
back, sending Mary catapulting through the air.

" I believe I've flown again," she said as she landed, a little
breathless, but safe, on quite a different tree.   Meanwhile the
man, awakened by the crack, got up, rubbing his eyes.   Looking up and seeing no sign of a bear he thought it must, after
all, have been a dream and, picking up his rope, he went off home.

Mary watched him out of sight and then crept cautiously down, dropped to the ground, and set off as fast as she could go in the opposite direction. Almost at once the trees ended and she found herself standing in a small street with houses on each side.

One house had a car standing outside—a car which reminded her of the Owl Man's. Cars meant travelling and svisits and picking nics and all kinds of nice things. Mary liked cars. She went up to this one and stroked it. No one was inside but there was a large black case strapped on behind, with a label on it.

Labels ! They meant travelling, too. But labels had to have writing on them and this was an empty one. " Labels, cars, travelling, Owl Man," thought Mary to herself. She began to smile and her smile grew bigger and bigger until it almost met behind. Then she bent down and began searching in the road. She had found a car and a label all ready for her and now all she wanted was a pencil and she felt quite sure she'd find one ready, too. She didn't, but a small piece of coal was just as good. Next she bit the string of the label through, and, kneeling down in the road, she wrote on it in Mary writing,

As coal isn't as easy to manage as a pencil, a good deal of it that didn't get on to the label got on to Mary. The writing finished, she searched for a place to put it, and, finding her ear seemed the most convenient place for a label, she tied it on there. At first she thought she would sit and wait and see what happened and then she thought it seemed a pity to waste the case, so she climbed up and got inside, but before she closed the lid she stood for a moment and said solemnly, " Mary Plain !   I bet you're going on a svisit after all ! "

CHAPTER FIVE

MARY WINS AGAIN

" Steady, there, whoa ! Let her down gently, Bill—that's right. Good ! I think you said you were the owner of this car, sir ? "

" That's right.   My suitcase is inside, but I've nothing to declare."

" What about the case on the back ? "

" Empty."

" Just let me have a look, please."

The man stepped forward, unfastened the catch, lifted the lid, gave one loud scream and fell down in a dead faint.

All the people standing on the pier at Dover immediately rushed forward, talking excitedly, asking each other what had happened, jostling and pushing towards the black case.   Out of the case rose Mary, very calm and dignified, in spite of affectionate bits of straw and a good deal of coal, still.   At sight of her, all the people who had been pressing forward began pressing backwards and, in a moment, there was an empty space round the car.

Mary gave a little bow; the label fluttered gaily from her ear.

"It's me," she said. "I'm Mary Plain, an unusual first-class bear from the pits at Berne and I won a white rosette and a gold medal with a picture of myself on it and I have come to svisit the Owl Man and I'm very empty. God save the King," she finished at the salute, remembering it was England.

Now, Mary had, of course, spoken in Swiss, so " God save the King " was the only thing that the crowd had understood, except for one man, who luckily had been to Switzerland and knew a little. Mary repeated, laying her hand with a great deal of feeling on the place, " I'm very empty here."

The man who understood Swiss took a step forward. " Hungry ? " he asked.

Mary nodded so hard that she nearly nodded herself out of the case. As this was the very last thing any of them wanted to happen the man said hastily, " You stop there and I'll fetch some milk and buns."

So Mary stopped and when the food arrived she tucked into it, while all the people stared and stared as if they had never seen a bear eat buns and milk before, which they probably hadn't. And while Mary ate and the people stared, all the officials discussed what to do with her.

Those in the Customs' Office were certain that the officials in the Lost Property Office ought to look after her and the Lost Property people felt quite sure it was the Customs' men's job. They were just going to toss for it when the head man suddenly said, "What about her passport? Has she got one? Otherwise she can't be allowed to land—she's not a British subject."

So the interpreter was pushed forward a step or two and he asked, " Have you got a passport ? "

" I don't think I have," said Mary, " but I've got some bathing drawers in Berne, with stripes—red and white."

This information, however, didn't seem to help the officials very much. " She oughtn't to land," said one. " It's against the law."

But Mary had landed and that was that, especially as no one seemed anxious to ask her to un-land.

Just at this point Mary, having finished her meal, stood up and beckoned to the man who had got it for her. Very naturally she looked on him as her greatest friend. The man was quite willing to be interpreter where he was, but he wasn't at all sure he wanted to be confidential close to—not with a bear. However, someone gave him a push again, and he went forward a few steps.

" Please," said Mary, " I'd like a bath."

Now, if she had asked for a bottle of champagne or even a Rolls Royce, it would have been less surprising and more convenient.

" A b–bath ! " stammered the man, turning pale and deciding on the spot that she was not only a loose bear but a mad bear, too.

" Certainly," said Mary, who was quite used to bathing in public. " You see," she continued, leaning confidingly over the edge of the case, " I'm a bit coaly and I don't like being called a hay-stack."

" H–hay-stack ! " repeated the man, more certain than ever that she was mad.

" So please will you get it for me ? " said Mary.

" Hot or cold ? " asked the man.

" Both," said Mary.

" Soap ? " asked the man.

" Pardon ? " said Mary, who didn't know about soap.

" Soap *and* towels ? " asked the man.

" Yes," said Mary, who never believed in saying ' No.'

And there and then, from somewhere, somehow, a tank of water was produced and there and then Mary had her bath in full view of the Dover public for, by this time, the news that there was a live bear loose on the pier had spread and everyone in the town was rushing to see her. As she climbed down from the case, the crowd all melted away behind a fence but, as she got into the water, first one and then another head came popping up to watch till there was a solid row of watching heads all along the fence. The water got blacker and blacker and Mary got cleaner and cleaner and when she had finished she got out and raced round and round to get dry and all the people of Dover were specially glad of the fence.

"What's that she's got on her ear?" asked one man as Mary flashed past, so, next time she came galloping along, they all craned their necks to see.

"Bless me if it isn't a label!" said the Head Customs' Officer. "Henry! Just get it for me, will you?" he called to the interpreter man.

But Henry didn't see why, just because he knew a little Swiss, he should be expected to get a label off a galloping bear and said so. Here the Officer got exceedingly angry and was just saying he would have to dismiss him for cowardice and shirking his duty, when Mary settled the question by turning a somersault, which loosened the label and sent it fluttering to the ground, close to the fence.

They fished it up with a stick and Henry was quickly called back so as to be able to translate. He stared at the label and scratched his head and said it was all gibberish to him and the Head Officer was just going to dismiss him again when a man pushed his way through the crowd. "Hallo!" he said, "what's all this about?"

The Officer handed him the label and the man exclaimed "Good heavens! If it isn't Mary writing!" and he read aloud

and then burst out laughing.

" Where is this bear ? " he asked and a way was cleared and he strode up to the fence and looked over. Mary was standing in the middle of the space looking her best, her fur and herself very sticking out and her pointed ears pricking, as she wondered what to do next.

" Hallo, Mary Plain ! " called the man and he vaulted over the fence, while all the crowd gasped and said, " He's got some nerve ! " " Remember me at all ? " went on the man. Mary trotted up to him and stared. " Weren't you one of the Fur Coat Lady's svisitors, when I went to stay with her ? " she asked.

" That's right ! Bill Smith's my name," said the man and Mary, the excitement of seeing someone she knew going to her head, hastily recited her list.

" I know all that," said Bill, " but look here, I'm off on this next boat in three minutes, and I must fly. I'll give them the Owl Man's address and they'll get hold of him for you. Good-bye, sit tight till he comes."

Mary immediately sat.

" Here, send a wire to this address," said Bill, thrusting a slip of paper into the Head Officer's hand and he rushed away.

Half an hour later the Owl Man who had just come in for a late lunch in a great hurry at his London flat, was handed a telegram.

" Important goods awaiting you here. Please collect at once."

It was signed by the Customs' Officer at Dover.

The Owl Man wired back, " Impossible come. Please seal goods and forward to above address."

But the answer came whizzing back along the wires.

" Impossible seal. Cannot approach. Dangerous. Come immediately."

And the Owl Man, angrily wondering who could have sent him a barrel of gunpowder, climbed into his car and started for Dover.

" This way, please, sir," said the Head Officer, more thankful to see him than he had ever been to see anyone in his life before, for the still growing crowd had blocked all the approaches to the pier and the Cross-Channel services threatened to be held up. And the Owl Man was led to the pier where Mary Plain was sitting as tightly as ever on exactly the same spot where Bill had left her.

" Gracious Heaven ! " said the Owl Man, standing stock still and staring at Mary as if he couldn't believe his eyes.

" I've come," said Mary, beaming all over.

" So I see ! " said the Owl Man, not beaming at all.

" Please could I stop sitting tight now ? " enquired Mary.

" Stop sitting tight ! What do you mean ? "

" The Bill man said I was to sit tight till you came and I have."

The Owl Man took a deep breath, shook his head, smiled and held out his hand.

" You win, Mary," he said, " as usual."

Mary, a little stiff, scrambled to her feet and tucked her paw into his hand.

" What have I won ? " she asked happily.

" Me," said the Owl Man and then, with a sigh, " as usual."

CHAPTER SIX

WHICH IS VERY MARY

" More porridge, Mary ? " asked the Owl Man, for the last time.

" Yes, please," said Mary.

He had quite decided this would be the last time because three times already he had said, " More porridge ? " and Mary had said, " Yes, please."

" That's all, now. You'll be eating me out of house and home, at this rate. To say nothing of getting too fat."

" ' Fat ' or ' flat,' did you say ? " asked Mary.

" ' Fat ! ' " said the Owl Man. " Good gracious me ! Show me any flatness about you, Mary Plain, and I'll give you a lump of sugar."

Mary, being very fond of sugar, stood up in her chair so as to get a good view of herself. The Owl Man had a good view, too—a profile one, against the sunny window and, as he saw it, he decided definitely, it must be two lumps. Mary shook her head sadly. " I'm afraid porridge isn't very flatting," she said, stroking the curve. " Perhaps there's a bit behind somewhere ? " she added hopefully and, climbing down, she presented her back to the Owl Man. " Please look."

The Owl Man looked. " Nothing doing, Mary," he said, " absolutely nothing, so I think you'd better have the sugar as a consolation prize, don't you ? "

" I bet," said Mary, crunching.

" The thing is," went on the Owl Man, " what on earth to do with you—you're immensely inconvenient just now, Mary."

" Is that a nice thing to be ? " enquired Mary.

" It's the sort of thing you very often are," said the Owl Man. " Well, I must be off, anyway. I've got a very important case on just now and I'm fearfully busy."

" Could I get inside ? " asked Mary, who was used to cases.

" It's not that kind," said the Owl Man, laughing. " No, you'll have to amuse yourself, Mary, as best you can, and I'll be back to lunch. Why don't you write to the bears and tell them where you are ? I expect they are all wondering. Look ! Here's some paper and pencils. Good-bye, be good," and off he went.

So Mary wrote :—

Here Mary paused a little to look round. The room was very empty, " There's only me," she thought.

WITH LVV ᕼ XXXXXXX
FROM 🐱 PLAIN

After another look round the room she wrote underneath :—

I HOP THE 🐱 🐱 R HAPPIE
WITHOUT M E
MARY

Then she got down.

" I don't like empty rooms," she said and, going to the hall door, she opened it quite easily because the Owl Man had forgotten to lock it, and running down lots of stairs, she found herself in a moment out in the street. That was empty too. " And," said Mary aloud, " I believe I'm beginning to be empty myself."

A sound of approaching music drew her down the street. Round the corner swung a band of ex-soldiers playing *Land of Hope and Glory*, but the next minute they caught sight of Mary and there isn't much glory about soldiers running away.

Next, Mary wandered up some front door steps and there was a nice shiny button there. Now shiny buttons always seemed to say " Please press me " to Mary, so she pressed, and went on pressing till the door was flung open by a very angry parlour-maid.

"Murder !" she exclaimed, suddenly seeing Mary and slamming the door in her face before Mary got a chance of explaining that she was not ' Murder ' but Mary.

Mary sat down disconsolately on the step to think over how very unfriendly people were, but she didn't sit there long for lots of other things began to arrive on the step too—hair brushes and books and bits of coal.

"This step doesn't seem to want me much," said Mary, getting up.

" Shoo, bear, go away, shoo ! " shouted a voice from above and Mary, looking up and receiving a glass of water full in the face, shooed.

Luckily she shooed back up the street and into the right door and into the lift and directly she shut the doors the lift began to go up, up.   Mary stared at the row of shiny buttons on the wall which said 1, 2, 3, 4, 5, 6. " I'm flying again," she thought, " me and the buttons together."

The lift stopped at the landing and Mary got out and found a lady and a little boy there.

First the lady screamed but Mary was used to this, and then she fell on her knees. " Mercy ! " she cried, clasping her hands together.   " Take me, but spare, oh ! spare, my little Harry ! Kneel, Harry, kneel ! " and she tried to pull Harry on to his knees.

But little Harry didn't want to kneel, he was far too inter ested in Mary.   Mary stared at the woman and wondered what she was saying and why she was on her knees.   Perhaps she had a pain ?

" Never mind," she said kindly, giving her a pat on the head, " you'll be better soon.   Try a hot sandbag."   And

she retired into the lift, and, because the shiny buttons winked
at her, Mary pressed and sailed down to the next floor.

"There, ducky! Just you wait and see what a treat
Nannie's got for her Baba this morning. She's going to take
her and show—her—"

But no one heard what Baba's treat was to be because just
as Nannie arrived at the treat, Mary arrived in the lift. Mary
hadn't any idea that anyone carrying a big baby could run so
fast—nor had Nannie, either.

Back in the lift, Mary pressed again and this time when she
stopped, the doors opened from the outside, so she tucked
herself into a corner to see what was going to happen. What

did happen was that a very plump old gentleman, shaking his head over all the noise going on above, got in, muttering, "Disgraceful! Might be a tenement—I shall lodge a complaint."

Mary could see he was very pink in the face. She waited till he had shut the doors and then she untucked herself, and because whenever she talked in Swiss, people seemed to disappear, she gave instead, her friendliest growl.

The old man seemed to turn to stone and then very stiffly and very slowly, he turned round and Mary saw, to her surprise, that his face wasn't pink after all but a kind of pale green. He stood there, staring at Mary with popping eyes, making swallowing noises. Mary, attracted by a large gold chain stretched across his waistcoat, bent forward and stroked it. The next moment the chain with a large gold watch at one end and a bunch of seals at the other, was in Mary's paw.

Meantime a crowd, led by little Harry and his self-sacrificing mother, Baba and Nannie, had collected and were all waiting at the bottom of the stairs for the lift to arrive, all ready to scream if Mary got out.

But she didn't. Instead, very slowly and backwards, came the plump old gentleman in his vest and trousers, while in the lift Mary, who adored dressing-up, was enjoying all the things she had stroked on the way down.

"Help!" thought the Owl Man, just back for lunch, and recognising a Mary scene at once. But a bit of fur in the lift caught his eye and the next minute he had shot into it, slammed the doors and pressed the button.

He stood with his back to the door and faced Mary. Mary was swamped in the plump old gentleman's shirt, her legs were thrust through the arm-holes of the waistcoat, while the gold watch sat perched on the top ledge of the porridge curve. But the Owl Man didn't seem to notice any of this. He only said grimly, " What next, Mary ? That's what I want to know. For pity's sake, what next ? "

" Dinner, I hope," said Mary.

CHAPTER SEVEN

ABOUT TWINS AND TELEPHONES AND A SHIPWRECK

FOR the next few days nothing very exciting happened, because the Owl Man was always most particular about locking the door before he went out.

In the afternoon he took Mary down to Richmond Park and she galloped about and chatted to the deer and enjoyed herself very much.

But she didn't enjoy the mornings at all. Every morning the flat seemed to get emptier and emptier till at last one morning, when the Owl Man came back, he found Mary so close to the door that he almost stepped on her as he opened it.

" Hallo ! " he said. " What are you up to ? "

But for once Mary wasn't up to anything. Instead she asked, in a very small voice, " Do you think the twins are happy without me ? "

" Oh dear," said the Owl Man, who knew something would have to be done at once.

" You see," said Mary, " there's always two of twins."

The Owl Man patted her head. " Quite right, Mary, but

I'm afraid I can't turn you into a twin, much as I'd like to please you."

"Could you buy me one?" asked Mary hopefully.

"I'm afraid not, but, come to think of it, I might borrow one—an English one."

"I'd rather have a Swiss twin, please," said Mary.

"No, an English one," said the Owl Man firmly, "and then you'll learn to speak the language. It won't be a bear, of course, but I might find a child who could come and play about with you."

"And be my twin?" insisted Mary.

"Well, you could always ask," said the Owl Man. "Hallo, that's the telephone."

"What are you talking into that little hole for?" asked Mary, who had followed him across the room.

"Ssh! Hallo, Jill, is that you? What? I'd love to. Right. I say, hold on a minute, there's a surprise for you here—a friend who wants a word with you. Here, Mary, it's the Fur-Coat-Lady."

Mary applied her eye to the hole. "It isn't!" she said reproachfully.

"No, no. You can't see her, only hear. Hold this up to your ear and put your mouth near the hole." Mary held the receiver and breathed heavily into the mouth-piece.

"Go on," urged the Owl Man encouragingly. "Say something."

"Something!" shouted Mary at the top of her voice.

"Steady, steady," said the Owl Man, "you don't have to shout," while the Fur-Coat-Lady at the other end wondered if her ear was broken.

" Isn't she in Switzerland, then ? " asked Mary.

By this time, and because of her ear, the Fur-Coat-Lady had guessed what the surprise was but, so as not to spoil it, she said, " Who *is* that, please ? " and Mary, hopping up and down with excitement, said, " It's Mary Plain, an unusual first-class bear with a—"

" Here, that'll do," said the Owl Man, removing the receiver. " Did you get that, Jill ? I say, couldn't you come round and have lunch ? Yes, now. Good ! We'll wait for you and afterwards we must have a Mary conference."

Mary sat down on a chair facing the telephone and the Owl Man left her there while he went off to see to something in his room. When he came back, Mary was still there and it was so unlike her to be still in the same place that he was just going to ask her if she was sure she felt quite well, when the doorbell rang.

" That will be the Fur-Coat-Lady, I expect," he said and went off to answer it.

It was, but when they came back Mary was still sitting with her eyes glued to the telephone. " Why doesn't she hurry up ? " she complained. " I'm so tired of her not coming."

" But I'm here ! " said the Fur-Coat-Lady.

Mary swung round and the next minute the Fur-Coat-Lady was getting a real Mary hug which is a particularly nice thing to get.

" But how did you come ? " asked Mary, looking first at the telephone and then at her friend. " I didn't see you come out. Was it a conjuring trick ? " And though they both explained hard, Mary couldn't really understand about telephones.

They had lunch and, as the Owl Man scraped the last of the suet pudding on to Mary's plate, he said, " Mary is a very unwasteful person to have about."

" So I see," said the Fur-Coat-Lady who had not seen Mary for some time and had forgotten about her appetite. " Don't you ever feel anxious ? " she asked.

" Four times a day, terribly ! " said the Owl Man. " I shudder to think what would happen if she should ever get punctured with a pin."

" Get what ? " said Mary.

" Get down and wipe your paws carefully," said the Owl Man.

After lunch they held the Mary conference and it was decided that the first thing to do was to teach Mary English. " And the best way to do that," said the Owl Man, " is to get hold of some child who could be with her. I know. A friend of mine in the flats above has a young god-son staying with him— the very thing. I'll run up now and see if I can arrange any-thing."

Presently he came back with a small boy. " This is Mark," he said. " He's lonely too, when he's not at school and, what's more, he can understand Swiss a bit, so you ought to get on like a house on fire, Mary."

Mary stared at Mark and Mark stared back, not quite sure whether you shook hands with a bear or not. Mary settled the question by going up to him and giving a little bow. " Will you be my twin when I want one, please ? " she said. And Mark, who knew his manners, bowed back and said he'd do his best.

" Well, as that seems to be satisfactorily settled, I must fly," said the Owl Man and flew.

" How would you like to go and see the boats on the Round Pond, you two ? " suggested the Fur-Coat-Lady.

" Is it a wet kind of pond ? " asked Mary, and when they said " Yes," she said she must just go and fetch her luggage.

The luggage had arrived that morning from Berne and was an exceedingly gaily checked bag with a zipp fastener but when Mark asked what was inside, Mary said it was very private luggage. The Fur-Coat-Lady thought she had never seen such un-private luggage in her life, but she didn't say so.

When they reached the Marble Arch they stood waiting to cross by a Belisha beacon and Mark, who didn't know Mary very well, said for fun, " Have an orange ? "

" Yes, please," said Mary, just as the policeman stopped the traffic for them to cross.

" Come on, Mary," said the Fur-Coat-Lady, pulling. But Mary braced her legs and said " After the orange," and the traffic jamb got bigger and bigger and the Fur-Coat-Lady pulled and the policeman shouted and then, just in time, Mark had a clever idea.

" There's some on the other side," he said and then, so as to make a sure thing of it, he added, " Nice big juicy ones," and Mary stopped bracing and crossed at once.

Safely on the other side, Mark explained that he had only been teasing her and Mary didn't like him quite so much as she had at first and, by the time she had climbed up the beacon to see for herself that it was a joke orange, and the policeman had taken the Fur-Coat-Lady's name and address for allowing her to climb the beacon, the usual crowd had collected.

" This won't do," said the Fur-Coat-Lady, rather pink in the face, and she called a taxi and bundled her charges in.

Luckily at the Round Pond there were only a few children, because it was a cold day. One of them was Sandy. Sandy was the Fur-Coat-Lady's nephew and Mary had met him when she was svisiting her.

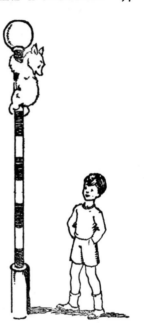

"Hallo, Mary," he called, while all the other children wished they knew a bear. "These are my two friends, David and Michael."

David and Michael were as like as two peas and Mary looked at them hard and then pulled the Fur-Coat-Lady's arm. She bent her head and Mary whispered "Why are they both the same ?"

"Twins !" whispered the Fur-Coat-Lady.

"Good morning, both !" said Mary, politely bowing. "This is my twin," and she pulled Mark forward. Mark, rather red in the face, translated and said, "It's only a game, of course."

The twins looked very envious.

"I wish I could have a little holiday from David and be Mary's twin instead," said Michael.

Among the other children Mary specially liked a small girl in a very blue bonnet and coat with eyes to match, because blue was Mary's ' best ' colour. She was called Ruth.

The small girl had a white steamer with a little wooden captain on board which chugged across the pond, while she

She picked up the captain in her mouth

stood on the edge and shouted " Look at my captain !   Just look at my captain ! "

But, alas, a big battleship ran right into the little white steamer and it was sunk, and the captain went down with his ship.   The ship stayed sunk but the captain floated to the top and the small girl wrung her hands and said, " Oh, won't somebody save me my captain ? "   And Mary, perhaps because she was so blue, decided she would.   Again she pulled at the Fur-Coat-Lady's arm.   " Please could you be a tree for a minute," she said, " because there isn't one near ? "

" Certainly," said the Fur-Coat-Lady, standing very stiff and hoping she looked like an elm, while Mary puffed and panted behind her and then came out dressed in her red and white bathing drawers.

She took a running dive into the Pond, and in a few moments, she was out at the scene of the disaster.   Here she dived again and again and came up spluttering and there was a lot of splashing and fuss while Mary seemed to be tying herself into knots under the water and then she picked up the captain in her mouth and started for shore.

Mary had gone into the water her usual shape but she landed quite another, and the Fur-Coat-Lady looked at the odd knobbly bulges which stuck out in front and wondered anxiously about bears' appendixes.   Anybody who knew Mary wasn't surprised about ordinary bulging but this was different, and a little alarming.

However, the children didn't seem to notice.   They stood in two rows and made an arch with their arms and Mary walked underneath, bowing to left and right and thoroughly enjoying the cries of " Well done, Mary Plain ! " which was the kind of English she could understand.   At the end of the arch stood Ruth who flung her arms round Mary's wet neck and cried, " Oh thank you, thank you, brave bear ! "   Being a bear, Mary, of course, couldn't blush, but she did feel very awkward with the small girl fastened round her neck like a necklace and was very glad when someone unfastened her.

She went at once to the Fur-Coat-Lady.   " Please will you be my tree again ? "   and once more the Fur-Coat-Lady played at being an elm.   This time there was a good deal of grunting and then a sound of popping elastic and then Mary emerged with the little white steamer in her hand and the right shape in front.   " Thank   goodness,"   said   the   Fur-Coat-Lady, fervently.

Then Mark climbed up on the railings and shouted, " Let's give her a bear cheer, everybody.   Come on ! "

And all the children cried, " Hip, hip, hoo-Mary !   Hip, hip, hoo-Plain ! " as loud as they could.

CHAPTER EIGHT

MARY SVISITS A DANCING-CLASS

MARY was getting on very nicely with her lessons. Mark went to school in the mornings and then she did lessons alone with the Fur-Coat-Lady, but after lunch Mark very kindly had another lesson with Mary as she seemed to learn much quicker if there was anyone about whom she had a chance of beating. Twice she had been at the top of the class which meant of course at the top of Mark.

Mary's dictations were quite different from Mark's. For instance the Fur-Coat-Lady would say, " The teapot was left in the kitchen."

Mark would write, " The teepot was left in the kittchen," but Mary would write it like this :—

THE 🫖 WAS LEFS IN THE 🐱 CHIN

The first morning the Fur-Coat-Lady and Mary had started off cheerfully on arithmetic but, at the end of the lesson, the only one that was cheerful was Mary. The Fur-Coat-Lady had a headache.

To start the arithmetic lesson she had emptied a box of matches on to the table. Mary had told her she could count up to 5 backwards or forwards, always, and up to 7 on extra clever days. This first day, however, didn't seem to be an extra clever day, and Mary stuck at 6. After that she said "lots of matches," or "heaps of matches," or just "more matches."

So the Fur-Coat-Lady, who knew Mary rather well, fetched a bowl full of lump sugar. Mary's eyes glistened. "Sugar's *much* easier to count," she said, and the Fur-Coat-Lady congratulated herself on having had such a very good idea.

"Now Mary, come along. One lump of sugar."

"One lump of sugar," repeated Mary as well as she could because of its being the biggest in the dish.

"Yes, this is a very good idea," thought the Fur-Coat-Lady, watching Mary's happy face. "This is the right kind of lesson for bears. When we do geography I shall have a saucer of milk for the seas and sugar for islands. Lessons ought to be fun."

Mary finished the lump carefully before she picked up another and popped that into her mouth. "One lump of sugar," she said again.

"No," said the Fur-Coat-Lady. "Two."

"But it's one," said Mary, "look!"

"That'll do, Mary," said the Fur-Coat-Lady, hastily, wondering if her idea had been such a good one after all. "But it is your second lump," she added.

Mary looked stupid. Mary could look very stupid if she liked and she did like now. She opened her mouth wide.

"That'll do," said the Fur-Coat-Lady again, trying not to see her tonsils.

" But there isn't anything there, is there ? " And the Fur-Coat-Lady was forced to admit there wasn't.

So Mary picked up another lump and looked at the Fur-Coat-Lady out of the corner of her eye—not a stupid look this time. " One lump of sugar," she said, as it disappeared.

" And now," said the Fur-Coat-Lady firmly, " we will have some geography," and she removed the sugar-bowl and, at the same time, gave up any idea of a milk Mediterranean because of the expense it would be.

" Perhaps, after all, you'd do better at school," she said, looking doubtfully at Mary.

" Oh, but I like these kind of lessons very much indeed, thank you," said Mary, licking her lips.

So the lessons continued and the Owl Man's sugar bill was enormous and the Fur-Coat-Lady said she was very sorry but he'd better try and teach Mary himself and then he'd see. But the Owl Man didn't a bit want to see and he paid the bill without another word.

Mary got on excellently well with her English, and one day the Fur-Coat-Lady said she was such a good pupil that she would give her a treat and take her to watch Sandy's dancing class.

The class was held in a large empty room and directly they went into it, Mary fell flat on her back.

" Oh dear," said the Fur-Coat-Lady, " it's slippery, like the rooms in my house. I ought to have warned you."

" You did," said Mary, rubbing her behind.

Now, it is very exciting and a little upsetting when a bear comes to watch you dance for the first time and the forty little girls in frilled skirts and thirty-five little boys in silk shirts, all kept their eyes fixed on Mary instead of on the dancing mistress.

So presently the mistress said that perhaps it would be better if the little visitor came and sat in front, and she pulled up two chairs for Mary and the Fur-Coat-Lady.

Mary gave a little bow before she sat down and the mistress said " Charming ! Now, children, what do little ladies do when a gentleman bows to them ? *All* together ! " And all the rows of little girls in frilled skirts curtsied to the ground. Mary was so impressed that she got off her chair and tried to curtsy back but it wasn't much of a success for somehow she trod on her own paw and fell. The kind mistress picked her up.

" I'm good at bowing," explained Mary, " but I'm not bendy here," and she laid her paw on the place where most people wear their waists.

" Quite," said the mistress helping her to her seat.

" And, please," said Mary, " I aren't a gentleman but a gentle-lady."

" I beg your pardon," said the mistress.

" Certainly," said Mary graciously. " Bears all dress the same, so it's very mixing, isn't it ? "

The mistress agreed and the Fur-Coat-Lady said Mary must really sit still and not interrupt any more. But Mary didn't sit still long, because very soon they started skipping. She got down at once.

" I always win at skipping, so could I try, please ? "

" Mary ! " said the Fur-Coat-Lady, getting very pink because of Mary's boasting but the mistress said, " Never mind,

I understand," and then " Aline and Gervase! Will you both swing a rope for our little visitor ? "

So Aline and Gervase swung and Mary, her paws tight down at her sides and her ears flying, jumped so high that they could pass the rope three times underneath before she came down.

" She's done the ' treble-through,' " said Aline in awed tones.

" Oh, it's very easy indeed," panted Mary, a little puffed by her jumping but more puffed at her success.

" Oh, Mary ! " said the Fur-Coat-Lady again.

" And now, how would you like to try to do some of the exercises ? " enquired the mistress.

" Please," said Mary, so a space was made in the front line between Aline and Gervase for her.

"Now, children! First position!" called the mistress.

All the little girls placed their feet neatly in the first position —right foot turned outwards. Mary, watching them, did her utmost to do the same.

The mistress passed along the front row, criticising. "Well done, Polly! Good, Felicity! Excellent, Joy and June!"

When she came to Mary and saw her right paw neatly in the first position, only inwards, she stopped. Mary looked up at her anxiously. She was trying terribly hard. "It fits better this way," she said, trying, without success, to see her own paws. "It's an excellent fit," said the mistress, kindly, and gave her a pat on the head.

Then came the final march and the mistress said would Mary care to join in and, of course, Mary cared.

"Let me see," said the mistress, holding Mary by the paw, "who had she better march with? I think Jenny would be the right height. Yes." She clapped her hands. "Will Jenny please come here?" And Jenny came, in a white frock with a blue sash and a blue wreath of flowers round her curls.

"I've got a blue bow at home," said Mary.

"Have you?" said Jenny, wondering where she wore it.

"I wish it was here," said Mary, looking wistfully at Jenny's wreath.

Jenny's Nanna rushed to the rescue. "Jenny likes marching without her wreath, don't you, Jenny?" she said brightly, and the next minute the blue wreath was round Mary's neck. Jenny gave a little sigh but, after all, what was the loss of a blue wreath and a few curls in the eye compared to marching with a bear, she told herself.

" Now, Jenny ! " said the mistress, " you two shall lead."
(" Leading too ! " thought Jenny.   " Bother the wreath ! ")
" Take her paw—so !   Now, children, point your toes."
Mary, with extreme difficulty, pointed her paw.
" Ready ?   One, two, three, march ! "
And round went all the forty frilled skirts and the thirty-five
silk shirts with Mary and Jenny in front, marching beautifully,
because of both having lots of hair and the same kind of shape.

Just as they got near the door, the Owl Man came in and,
seeing the approaching procession, he tried to slip behind
someone.

But it was very difficult to slip with Mary about.   " Hallo ! "
she shouted, delightedly, coming to a halt and bringing all the
marching children into a jamb behind her.   " Jenny and me's
leading, both of us.   Look at my points ! "

" Get on, Mary," urged the Owl Man.   " Don't stop,
go on ! "

But Mary wanted to tell him all about what she had been
doing and the Owl Man, because it was the only thing to do,
took her paw and marched along beside her, very much wishing he had stayed behind with his case.

The music ended, the children crowded round Mary and
the mistress came up and thanked the Owl Man for saving the
situation.

" What's a situation ? " asked Mary.

" Well, you ought to know better than most people," said
the Owl Man, putting his hand on Mary's head to stop her
jumping.   " Time you came home, Mary.   There's altogether
too much bounce about you to-day."

" It's a bouncy kind of day," said Mary.

" Look at my points ! "

"Most of your's are," said the Owl Man, as he led her away.

"Come again, come again!" shouted all the children, who had found dancing classes with bears far more fun than without.

"All right!" shouted Mary back. "And next time I'll do the 'sixle-through.'"

CHAPTER NINE

MARY GOES TO SCHOOL

THE great day came when Mary was to go to school for the first time with Mark. He went to a senior class, of course, but Mary was to go to the Kindergarten where the very smallest children were.

She had passed the entrance exam with flying colours. One or two of the teachers weren't at all sure that some of Mary's answers were not too flying, but they all agreed that she showed promise. Here are the exam questions, with Mary's answers underneath.

1. *Why do you want to come to school?*
   To get to the top of the class.
2. *What is the difference between a pond and a lake?*
   A pond is wet and a lake is wetter.
3. *How do you spell physic?*
   I don't.

4. *When do you feel happiest ?*
Eating meringues.

5. *When do you feel saddest ?*
Finishing meringues.

6. *Name three famous people.*
Mary Plain, Mary Plain, Mary Plain.

7. *Who is your favourite saint ?*
St. Bruin.

8. *Name two kinds of wool.*
Big and Little.

9. *What do the following letters stand for—L.s.d., G.R. ?*
Because there isn't a chair to sit on.

And the examining mistress had written underneath *Passed on the last answer.*

Mark came down after breakfast to see if Mary was ready.

" Has she got her satchel ? " he asked the Owl Man.

" Rather," said the Owl Man, " time to get ready, is it ? "

" Yes. I'll just run up and get my things on and then I'll come and fetch you, Mary."

" I'll be quite ready," promised Mary, trotting off to her room with the satchel. She was ! When Mark came back, she came trotting back again, looking as pleased as Punch.

" Phew ! " said the Owl Man and " Oh, I *say !* " said Mark, beginning to wonder if he wouldn't rather Mary went to school separately.

" I've been getting my things on too," she said.

" You have ! " said the Owl Man.

For Mary had on her red and white bathing drawers, her blue bow, and her gold medal and chain. Down the back hung the card she had had at the Crystal Palace Show with

" Miss Mary Plain. From the famous Bear Pits at Berne. Shown by the Owl Man," written on it and, as a final touch, she had pinned the white rosette on to the front of the bathing drawers. She held the satchel in her paw.

" There doesn't seem to be any room for this," she said.

" There doesn't, does there," said the Owl Man helplessly, wondering how he could get the things off.

" I must be smart for school," said Mary, preening herself.

" Yes. But not *too* smart," said the Owl Man, seeing Mark's face of growing horror and pulling himself together. " You must just let me explain. You see, Mary, you couldn't possibly wear your medal, for instance, because all the children would want medals too, and bathing drawers are absolutely forbidden in the autumn term, aren't they, Mark ? "

" Absolutely," said Mark, firmly.

" And this card," went on the Owl Man, and presently he had explained all the things off and there was only Mary left. She stood, drooping a little, and looking sadly at the pile of things on the table.

" All the smart has gone now," she said and her voice wobbled. " Do you think the twins are happy without me ? "

And the Owl Man said, very loudly and cheerfully, " Oh, but we've forgotten her school colours, Mark ! She can't possibly go to school without her colours. I've got the ribbon somewhere. Now, where did I put it ? " and he went on loudly and cheerfully hunting for the ribbon.

" Would she like my cap, just for to-day ? " suggested Mark, feeling sorry for Mary who looked as if she was still thinking about the twins.

So they tried the cap on, first on each ear and then between, but it was no good, Mary just didn't suit caps.

" No, it will have to be a bow," said the Owl Man, " Mary wears a bow very well."

" I'm glad I wear something well," said Mary a trifle bitterly.

" Or what about a belt ? " suggested Mark. " I say, wait a sec." and he fiddled in his pocket and produced a school belt, complete with a snake buckle, " I thought so—the very thing."

" Always providing we find just the right position and that it fits," said the Owl Man, shutting one eye and looking at Mary. After a bad shot or two he found the position but, alas, there were three good inches of Mary between the two ends of the belt—four when she breathed.

The Owl Man shook his head and pursed his lips and did a good deal of fiddling with the belt and tried again and this time there was a most satisfactory little click as the buckle snapped together.

She marched off between them

"Luckily for you it was a very obliging snake," said the Owl Man, mopping his brow and stepping back. "Yes, there's no doubt about it, that was a very good suggestion of yours, Mark. Mary wears a belt exceedingly well—exceedingly well."

"Yes," agreed Mark. "You look terribly smart, Mary. Got your lunch?"

Mary dropped her eyes and looked at the floor.

"Have you, Mary?" asked the Owl Man, suddenly suspicious.

Mary kicked at the floor a bit with her paw and the Owl Man got up and looked inside the satchel. "There were three bananas and two *Petit Beurre* biscuits in this satchel this morning, weren't there, Mary?"

"Yes," said Mary, still kicking at the floor.

"And where are they now?"

"Inside me," said Mary, who was often truthful.

The Owl Man didn't speak but his back view, as he went off to collect a second lunch, was very expressive.

At last Mary was ready, with her satchel strapped on her back, and she marched off between them, one arm stretched very high because of the Owl Man being so tall.

"I'll just come in and introduce you," he said and, when they got to Mary's class-room, they found a nice surprise waiting for them, for the teacher was the lady in the blue hat whom they had met in the Golden Arrow train on Mary's last visit to England.

"Blue is still my best colour," said Mary frankly.

"That's good," said the lady, "because it's still mine, as you see by my jumper."

" Yes," said Mary, wondering if it ever jumped.

" Now, children, this is Mary Plain and you must all be very kind to her because this is her first day at school."

" Yes," said all the children, staring hard at Mary as they sat at their little desks.

" This is your desk, Mary, between Prudence and Nicholas, just behind Richard. Come and sit down." But Mary got rather badly stuck in her effort to sit and then it was discovered that she still had her satchel on. The mistress took it off and wanted to take it away but Mary said " It's mine, it's mine ! " and grabbed at it. " Very well," said the teacher sensibly, " we'll put it by your feet and, so it won't get lost, you shall write your own name on a label and stick it on. That will give you something to do while I am correcting these exercises. Look, here are some sticky labels," and she handed Mary a little book of labels. Mary pulled one out, wrote on it and then licked it.

Then she licked her lips. "This is a nice label," she thought. "I'll just see if the next one tastes the same."

When the teacher came back, there were no labels in the little book but Mary's satchel had a white coat on. It looked like this.

"Everyone can see it's mine now, can't they?" said Mary.

"Unless they were quite, quite blind," agreed the teacher, knowing she ought to scold Mary but not doing it because of its being her first morning at school. So instead she fetched out a huge cardboard clock and, hanging it up at the end of the room, she began moving the hands round and asking the children to tell the time.

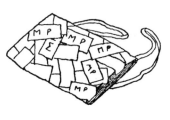

"What's that?" she asked.

"Eleven!" said one child.

"Quite right! We all know eleven, Mary, because that is the time we have our lunch." Mary's ears pricked. The next time it pointed to eleven Mary shouted "Banana time!" and all the children laughed.

When banana time really came, Mary was the centre of a crowd, but she was too busy with her bananas and *Petits Beurres* at first to talk much and when she was ready to talk the bell rang for dictation.

Mary, as usual, did well at the dictation and when they had finished the teacher said that, to end up with, they could each try and write a little poem.

"A pome about what?" asked Mary.

" Anything you like, as long as it is really interesting," said the teacher.

So Mary wrote :—

> *I dance like a fairy*
> *I'm lovely and hairy*
> *I went in an airy*
> *O plane.*

> *I am a bear*
> *A famous bear*
> *My name is Mar*
> *Y Plain.*

The teacher didn't know what to say when she had read Mary's. It was definitely a boasty poem and she ought not to allow boasty poems but, on the other hand, she couldn't help agreeing with Mary that Mary Plain was a very interesting subject to write about. So she got out of it by saying that the poem was a little unusual and that she would have to take it home and think over how many marks it deserved.

And that evening Mary told the Owl Man that they had been asked to write a poem about something interesting. " And guess what mine was about ! " said Mary, hopping up and down in front of him. " You can have three guesses."

" I shall only need one," said the Owl Man.

CHAPTER TEN

WHEN Mary had been at school about a fortnight, one of the children in the Kindergarten developed measles.

"We are not going to close the school," the Head Mistress wrote to the Owl Man, "as we hope there will be no further cases, but I would be glad if you would keep an eye on Mary Plain as, of course, she has been exposed to the infection."

So every morning before he went off to his case the Owl Man had a Mary inspection.

"Tongue out," he ordered and Mary hung her tongue out so far that every day it was a fresh surprise to him. "Feel all right?" he would then ask and Mary would say, "Quite, thank you," and the inspection would be over.

But one morning Mary's tongue, though it was just as long, wasn't a nice tongue and when, with a sinking heart, the Owl Man asked her how she felt, she said her throat felt tight. So the Owl Man telephoned at once to a doctor friend of his who had a small children's hospital and explained about Mary and the doctor said he'd better bring her round at once and let him have a look at her; luckily there was a vacancy in the measles ward, so, if necessary, Mary could be kept there.

On the way down in the lift Mary was so quiet that the Owl Man said "Feeling all right, Mary?"

"My head hurts," said Mary and the Owl Man wished lifts weren't so slow.

As they got into the car Mary said, "My head hurts more," and the Owl Man drove as fast as he dared till a traffic block held them up and he came to a dead stop.

"I feel sick," said Mary helpfully.

"Well, you can't be sick now, Mary," said the Owl Man, desperately, "not in my new car. You must hang on till you get to the hospital."

"I'll try," said Mary. And the Owl Man put the accelerator down very hard and did all the things one oughtn't to do in London, like cutting in and taking no notice of Belisha crossings, and in five minutes he was at the hospital. It was a tall black house and Mary, after one look, said, "My head is better and my sick has all gone now and if I have to have measles I'd rather have them at home with you, thank you."

"I'm afraid that isn't possible," said the Owl Man. "You see, I'm away at my case all day and bears can't have measles alone in flats—it isn't done. No, if it is measles you'll be far better off here, Mary, and, perhaps, after all, it's not that at all. We'll see!"

But that was just what the doctor couldn't do.

"I'm afraid we shall have to—well—clear the ground a bit," said Dr. Murphy.

"Quite," said the Owl Man.

So a razor was fetched and a small neat square made on Mary's chest and inside the square they found the measles.

" So that's that ! " said Dr. Murphy. " Now, I must just fill up this card—a mere question of formality." And he did a bit of questioning and the Owl Man did a bit of answering and then the doctor handed over a card on which was written,

> *Name, Christian*   Mary.
> *Surname (in block capitals)*   PLAIN.
> *Profession*   Svisiting spinster.
> *Address*   Bear Pits, Berne.
> *Nature of ailment*   Measles (mild).

Across the bottom was printed in red letters,
> *Please admit bearer to Sunshine ward, Bed* 27.

" Have I won a prize ? " asked Mary.

" Not this time, old girl," said the Owl Man. " This is just a kind of invitation from Dr. Murphy asking you to svisit him for a little while. He's a great friend of mine and I'm sure he'll be glad to help you if he can. She's never been in hospital before and—well, you understand, Murphy ? "

" Perfectly," said Murphy. " If there's anything you want, Miss Plain, just let me know. And now, if you'll take her up to the ward—third floor and the lift's at the end of the passage —I'll be up presently to have a look at her." Mary went off, holding very tightly to the Owl Man's hand.

Sunshine Ward was full of measly children. Some extremely measly, some only a little, but none too measly to be interested in Mary's arrival. A nice young nurse came smiling to the door.

" I'm afraid I can't let you come any further," she said to

the Owl Man. " You see, this is an infectious ward. She is to have the bed in the corner—I'll just turn back the cover."

The nurse went off and the Owl Man looked down at Mary. She looked very small and clung to his hand more tightly than ever.

" Well, Mary," he said, in an extra cheerful voice, " I must be off."

" Please," said Mary, earnestly, " I'm quite sure the measle has gone now. Just you look."

The Owl Man bent and examined the square. Then he shook his head. " Afraid not, Mary. But cheer up, you'll be so happy here, you won't want to leave when the time comes ! Here comes your nurse. Do you see she has a blue dress on ? Specially for you, I expect," he whispered encouragingly.

But Mary wouldn't be encouraged. " I wish it was pink," she said unreasonably and holding on to him with both paws. Luckily, the Owl Man hadn't been Mary's friend for a year for nothing. Just as the nurse came back, he whipped a little parcel out of his pocket and slipped it into her paw.

" There ! " he said. " That's to open when you're in bed," and before Mary could say another word he had disappeared.

Five minutes later Mary was sitting up in bed, in a red flannel bed-jacket a size too big for her, eating a bowl of bread and milk and opening the parcel between the mouthfuls. Presently Dr. Murphy came along and got out his stethoscope to listen to her chest.

" Why are you telephoning me for ? " asked Mary.

" Because there are one or two things I want to ask you," said the doctor. " You've got a headache, you said. Is that all ? "

" I feel prickly," said Mary. " It prickles me to sit."

" H'm. Any other symptoms ? "

" Symp—what ? " said Mary.

" Toms," said the doctor. " Feelings, I mean."

" Oh yes," said Mary, " I feel quite sure I'd be better at once if I could go home to the Owl Man."

" Well, I didn't quite mean that," said the doctor kindly, " I meant aches or pains."

" I feel achy here," said Mary, pointing to her left side.

" Yes, that's a very usual sort of ache to have on the first day," said Dr. Murphy, " and, luckily, one I'm sure we can quickly cure. Well, good-night to you, Miss Plain. Remember, if there's anything you want, you have only to ask."

Mary asked for a good deal before the nurse got her settled

for the night. She asked three times more for bread and milk and the nurse, who had never nursed a bear before, got it for her and then she asked for a basin and the nurse said she wasn't at all surprised. At seven o'clock nurse went off duty and left all the children tucked up for the night. Each had a little bell beside their bed ; she said she hoped they wouldn't use it but it was for the night nurse—just in case.

In Mary's case it was most useful. The bell got little rest that night, nor did the nurse.

The first time Mary rang it because she wanted to hear what kind of noise it made.

The second time she rang it she asked for bread and milk.

The nurse was firm—no bread and milk till morning.

Mary bore it for half-an-hour and then she rang again, this time keeping her paw on the bell till the nurse appeared.

" I want Dr. Murphy," said Mary, sitting up in bed, with a ruffled head and forgetting to say ' please.'

The nurse argued and Mary argued and Mary won. In tenminutes Dr. Murphy appeared in pyjamas with an overcoat on top. He looked very sleepy and not quite so kind as before.

" Hallo ! " he said. " What's all this about ? "

"Do youthink the twins are happy without me ? " said Mary.

" Bless my soul ! " said Dr. Murphy, sitting down rather suddenly. " Do you mean to say that you've got me out of my bed to ask me that ? Who are the twins, anyway ? " Mary explained and the doctor did his best to forget about his bed and to pacify her, remembering what the Owl Man had said about its being her first visit to a hospital. He left her with a pat on the head and an injunction to sleep tight till the morning.

Mary fell asleep for an hour.   Directly she woke, she rang the bell.   The nurse appeared.

"I want Dr. Murphy," said Mary.

"Oh no you don't," said the nurse, trying to forget what Dr. Murphy had said the last time she had woken him up.

But Mary won again.   Back came the doctor, looking less kind than ever.

"Look here, Miss Plain," he said, "I've had about enough of this."

"So have I," said Mary.   "I want the twins and the Owl Man and the Fur-Coat-Lady and my luggage and I've got a hurt in my head and my measles keeps waking me up and I'm not allowed any bread and milk and—"

"Oh, give her a bucket of bread and milk!" said Dr. Murphy and went back to bed.

CHAPTER ELEVEN

THE FIRE THAT WASN'T

THE next two days were very miserable ones for Mary. They moved her into a ward by herself. She tossed about in bed and her head ached and her body prickled; she even turned away from bread and milk, which was the worst sign of all.

But after a few days there was a distinct change for the better and she was able to sit up and take notice again. She listened in to the Children's Hour and very much enjoyed it.

" I'll give you a nice blanket bath," said nurse that evening. " It will make you feel clean and fresh." So she fetched a big basin of hot soapy water and put it by Mary's bed and then covered her up with blankets while she ran off to fetch a towel.

She seemed to be gone rather a long time and Mary, looking at the basin, thought it seemed a pity to waste any more minutes, so she threw off the blankets and climbing on to the table, got into the basin. It was a full basin and there wasn't

room in it for Mary and the water so most of the water went
on to the table and the floor.   Mary started rubbing herself
with what was left and made such a lovely lather that when
the nurse came back she looked like a picture of a small polar
bear, sitting in a lake.

"Gracious goodness ! " said the nurse, angry about the
wetness, but at the same time thinking how becoming the soap
was to Mary.   "Whatever are you doing, Mary ? "

" Just helping you to bath me," explained Mary, blowing
a soap bubble off the tip of her nose.   "Wasn't it kind of me ? "

The nurse didn't answer but she looked a lot.   She finished
Mary off and got her back to bed as quickly as she could.

"Now," she said, " I'll take your temperature and then
you can have a bowl of bread and milk.   Not that you deserve
it," she added.   She tucked the thermometer under Mary's
arm, and at the same time placed a steaming bowl by the
bedside.

" Don't you dare move for three minutes," she cautioned
Mary as she went off.

Mary lay and sniffed at the bread and milk.   Some sifted
sugar lay on the top.   It seemed a pity to leave it lying on the
top because it would taste better mixed.   But nurse had
forgotten the spoon.   "Never mind," thought Mary, " I'll
give it a mix with my 'mometer and then it'll be ready when
I want it."   So she did.

Back came nurse and whipped out the thermometer
from under her arm.   "Gracious goodness ! " she said again,
for Mary's temperature was about as high as it could go, and
she sat down rather suddenly on the bed and went the same
colour that the old plump man in the lift had gone.   "Don't

move, Mary, don't move an eyelid, till I fetch Doctor Murphy." She rushed off and Mary lay as still as a mouse, managing the eyelids very well but not so successful over her nose which would keep twitching because of the nearness of the milk.

Dr. Murphy came running. He felt Mary's pulse, looked at her tongue, telephoned her chest and pummelled her tummy.

" And now can I have my bread and milk, please ? " asked Mary. The doctor looked at the bread and milk, then at Mary and then at the thermometer and took a deep breath. " Only I haven't got a spoon," said Mary.

" So I see," said the doctor shortly. " So ought anyone to to see," he added, glaring at the nurse, whose face was now scarlet, " but some people don't use their eyes or their brains," and he stumped off angrily.

" Why did he look like that for ? " enquired Mary.

" Oh, why did you get measles for ? " answered the nurse impatiently.

" Not on purpose," said Mary trying to look offended and eat her bread and milk at the same time and not succeeding very well.

The supper finished, nurse tucked her up for the night.

" You just go to sleep and stay there, Mary Plain," she said, " we don't want to hear another sound from you till morning. Don't you forget it."

So when Mary woke up in the middle of the night and felt bored, she didn't ring her bell as usual but got out of bed, instead.

" I'll just have a bit of explore," she said, " and see what I can find."

She crept out of the room and into the big ward where she had been the first night. All the children were asleep, making soft breathing noises, not a bit like the bears' night noises. One little boy was lying on his back with his mouth wide open.

"Poor little boy," said Mary to herself, "he looks so thirsty," and picking up a glass of water, she emptied it into his mouth.

The boy sat up making loud spluttering and choking noises and the nurse came rushing through the door. Mary popped under the bed. "Perhaps it wasn't water he wanted," she thought, edging away from nurse's feet which kept poking under the bed and hoping she didn't show the other side.

"Must have dreamt you were thirsty, I should think!" said the nurse, as she bustled the boy into dry pyjamas while Mary, underneath, held her breath till she nearly burst.

At last all was quiet and Mary, rather stiff from her cramped position, crept out and tip-toed to the further door. It had been cold on the floor—linoleum isn't at all comforting to sit on. Mary shivered a little and looked back at the ward grate which was mostly grey ashes now with just a few little sparks left in one corner. " I wish I had a fire," she said disconsolately and, turning round, found the answer to her wish. For, hanging on the wall, just above her head, was a beautiful brass fire-helmet and underneath was a handle which said " Fire ! Pull ! "

So Mary pulled.

There was a loud whirr and then all through the hospital a deafening sound of electric bells, a sound that went on loudly and without stopping. It didn't even stop when four doctors, eleven nurses and nine maids came rushing up the stairs, carrying buckets of water and sand and all shouting different orders. " Where is the fire ? Someone locate the fire ! Clear the wards ! Women and children first ! "

Dr. Murphy sprang on to a chair and shouted through a megaphone. " Steady now, remember the children ! Half of you go down to the next floor and clear those wards. We must not let one little life be lost. Their safety comes first ! Open that window ! Let down the ladder escape ! Now, all of you, follow me ! " And picking up a measly child and flinging it, wrapped in a blanket, over his shoulder, the brave man sprang to the open window. Out on the sill he turned and shouted, " Don't spare the water. Remember, anything that's really wet has less chance of catching fire." Mary immediately emptied a bucket of water over the nearest nurse and then, as everyone seemed to be too busy rescuing children to follow the doctor's orders, she methodically emptied a bucket of water over each bed.

In a few moments she was alone in the ward, still working steadily. Going into the hall to fetch another bucket, her eyes fell on the brass fire-helmet, still hanging on the wall, all shiny and inviting. Climbing up, she got it unhooked just as a sort of roar went up from the yard outside, where all the rescued children and their rescuers were standing in different stages of shiver.

Mary listened. Whatever could they be shouting? Something about " volunteers " it sounded like. She ran back into the ward; her eye caught a little flicker still in the grate —mustn't leave that. Half of the bucket put it out and she didn't need the second half. It was the matter of a moment to empty it out of the window.

Screams and yells were now added to the shouting and some of the shouts seemed to be about " Mary Plain." It was time she went. She climbed out of the window. It was a little

A bit wobbly, because of the helmet

difficult to see as the brass helmet fitted her like an extinguisher. A roar greeted her appearance, she waved her paw airily. " It's all right," she called, " I've just put the fire out."

A second and louder roar greeted this remark and was continued while Mary descended the ladder (a bit wobbly because of the helmet being so much heavier than she was). At the bottom she was surrounded, patted, kissed, thumped on the back and carried shoulder high round the yard.

Half an hour later, seated on top of Dr. Murphy's desk, still in the helmet with two paws dangling and the other two busy with very sugary bread and milk, she gave a big contented sigh.

" We really are most deeply indebted to you, Miss Plain," said Dr. Murphy, as he handed her the sugar-bowl for the third time.

" In—what ? " asked Mary.

" Indebted—grateful."

" Oh, but it wasn't full," said Mary, " half a bucket was enough to put it out."

Dr. Murphy looked at her a little anxiously. " I hope the strain has not been too excessive ? " he said. " Perhaps you had better go to bed now ? "

" Perhaps I better had," agreed Mary, " me and the sugar-bowl. That's tired, too."

CHAPTER TWELVE

MARY GOES TO THE CINEMA

ON the day after she got back from the hospital, Mary was to give a welcome home party to which the Fur-Coat-Lady was to come. The Owl Man went off to his case as usual, a little uneasy about leaving Mary alone.

"You quite understand, Mary, that you will only have the party if you are very good?" he said. "It's a pity that it's a Saturday and there's no school. What will you do all the morning?"

"Oh, I've got lots to do," said Mary, "I shall be very busy being glad about getting home again."

The Owl Man laughed and patting her on the head went off, carefully locking the door behind him. Just after he had gone, the telephone bell rang. Mary went across the room and looked at it and then, as it still went on ringing, she picked up the receiver, rather gingerly.

"It's me," she said.

" This is the Ideal Bakery speaking. We understand that there is to be a party at your flat this afternoon and as the boy is just off with the bread, I thought I would ring and ask if you needed anything else sent along by him ? "

" What kind of things ? " enquired Mary.

" Well, scones or cakes or things in that line."

" Just the line I like," said Mary.

" Would you care for some cream buns ? They're nice and fresh this morning." Mary licked her lips.

" Yes, please," she said.

" How many dozen shall I send ? " enquired the woman. " Eight," said Mary, who had no idea what dozen meant.

" Eight dozen cream buns," said the woman, writing it down on her pad. " And some big cakes ? Lemon—coffee —orange—chocolate ? "

" Yes, especially chocolate," said Mary.

" Any éclairs ? "

Mary dribbled a little into the telephone. " Oh, yes, plenty of éclairs."

" Four dozen éclairs," wrote the woman. " And how about meringues ? "

" Oh, yes, please, more of meringues than anything else, please," said Mary.

" Ten dozen meringues," wrote the woman.

Some time later a bell rang again. It was the front door this time and the front door was locked so Mary could do nothing about it.

" I can't open it, it's locked, whoever you are," she shouted.

" It's the things from the bakery—shall I leave them outside ? "

" Yes, please," said Mary. How terrible not to have a key !

" I'll put the meringues down and go back for the rest," said the boy.

Mary bent down and sniffed through the keyhole. The boy came back several times and each time Mary heard exciting paper-rustling noises and said to herself " Éclairs, chocolate cake, cream buns, and no key ! Oh *dear !* "

The Owl Man could hardly reach the door when he got back—it was covered with paper bags. He had to wade knee deep through the pile to reach the keyhole. As he opened the door Mary fell out, right on to a bag of meringues which went off with a pop.

" What does this mean ? " asked the Owl Man angrily.

" What ? " asked Mary getting up with a good deal of burst meringue on her front which she proceeded to lick off.

" This—this—sea of confectionery."

" I don't see any sea," said Mary, " I can only see things for tea."

" Things for tea ! Who ordered them—how did they get here ? "

" The woman asked and I said ' Yes ' and the boy came," said Mary, going on licking.

The Owl Man strode to the telephone. Mary stayed behind, tidying up the meringues, so she didn't hear what he said but in a few moments the boy came running up the stairs very quickly and removed all the bags except three.

" Hallo, there's a bag of meringues missing," he exclaimed.

Mary tucked her paw, in which was a screwed up paper bag, behind her back.

" Meringues ? " she said innocently. " What are they like ? "

" White and crisp and—well—kind of full of cream," explained the boy.

" Well, I don't see any about, do you ? " asked Mary.

" Not exactly," said the boy, looking suspiciously at a damp spot on Mary's chest.

" So good-morning," said Mary, not liking the look, and she shut the door in his face.

The tea-party went off very well and afterwards the Owl Man said, " How about a cinema ? There's a rather primitive one round the corner but it's got the *Three Little Pigs* on and a couple of stars in something after."

Both the Fur-Coat-Lady and Mary said they'd like to go, so after tea they set off, Mary hopping a good deal because of never having been to a cinema before. There was some difficulty in getting her through the turnstile and finally the man kindly lifted her over the top.

It was quite dark in the theatre and they followed the attendant's flash lamp which guided them to their seats.

" Is that one of the stars we've come to see ? " whispered Mary, who had been told she mustn't talk out loud.

" No," said the Owl Man, fumbling in the dark. " Here, sit down, Mary, and be careful because it's a spring seat."

They had got there in such good time that it was the tail-end of the performance before and in a few moments the King's head appeared on the screen. Mary sprang to her feet. " God save the King," she said, at the salute.

"Sit down, Mary," said the Owl Man, wishing Mary was not quite so patriotic.   Mary sat, with a bump.

"Ow!" she said, "my seat's not there."

The Owl Man lifted her back.   "Now, for goodness sake, keep still, will you?"   And for a bit Mary did sit quite still, making whispered remarks about everything on the screen. The Fur-Coat-Lady decided that she had quite the loudest whisper of anyone she knew.

Some advertisements were shown.   A young lady tripped on to the screen and said, "Have you tried Clenolux?   Makes white things whiter still.   May one of our assistants call on you and show you her Clenoluxed blouse?"

Nobody answered so Mary, who felt rather sorry for the girl, called, " Do ! I'm always back from school by one."

" Shut up, Mary," said the Owl Man.

Next a man in a very waisted coat and patent leather hair stepped forward, holding a banner in his right hand on which was written *Worth & Co. General Furnishers. Established 1885. Worth we are and worth we supply.*

" Does anyone here want a free gift ? " he asked.

" I do," said Mary, quickly.

" Because if they do," continued the man, who didn't seem to have heard Mary, " come to our Jubilee party on Wednesday next. This is a Jubilee year. All tastes catered for, at all prices. Come and see."

" I will," promised Mary.

Then came a picture of a very fat man under which was written *January*, 1934, followed almost immediately by one of the same man, looking beautifully flat and labelled *January*, 1935. Underneath was written in scarlet letters. *Try our Fitite belt.*

" That might suit you, Mary," whispered the Owl Man, giving Mary a nudge.

" But I've got a belt already," objected Mary, not seeing the joke.

Chocolates and ices will be served in the interval, said the screen.

" Where's the interval ? " asked Mary, pulling the Owl Man's arm and preparing to get up.

" It's here," said the Owl Man. " If you sit tight and keep quiet, it won't be long."

But you might just as well ask Niagara to stop Niagging.

From then on Mary's conversation was something like this. " Has the interval come yet ? Why has he got black hair on his chin ? What kind of ices will they be ? I like pink ones best. Why is she taking her dress off ? Who's that in the bath ? Wouldn't it be lovely to have a bath of ice-cream ? Why is he squeezing her neck like that for and why is he putting her into a trunk ? " The Owl Man gave up saying ' Hush ', it just wasn't any good.

At last the interval came and the attendant came along with a tray of ices. The interval was the only time that Mary was silent. Luckily, there weren't many people in the cinema and none of them seemed to mind Mary except one bald man who made hissing noises through his teeth from time to time.

The *Three Little Pigs* came next and when they cried, " Whose afraid of the Big Bad Wolf ? " Mary shouted, " I'm not," but when the Big Black Wolf came galloping towards them, growing bigger and bigger till he burst off the screen at them, Mary disappeared under the Owl Man's chair and there she remained, gripping each ankle, which was very inconvenient for him and rather tickling.

" Come along, Mary," he said, hoping there wouldn't be a fire, so he'd need his ankles.

" I like it best here," said Mary, and there she stayed till half-way through *Golden River* when the Owl Man came to the conclusion he couldn't bear a moment's more tickling and they all went home.

As he was tucking Mary up in bed that night, she said, " What does ' Jubilee ' mean ? "

" It means a kind of special birthday. The King is having one this year to celebrate his twenty-five years' reign."

" Did he come to the cinema especially to see me this afternoon ? "

" Very likely," said the Owl Man.

" How did he know I was there ? " asked Mary.

" Must have guessed," said the Owl Man. " They say he's very unusual."

" That makes two unusual people in one cinema," said Mary, drowsily. " Me and the King."

CHAPTER THIRTEEN

IN WHICH MARY GOES JUBILEEING

FOR weeks Mary had been talking about the Jubilee and when the day actually came she was up and dressed and calling the Owl Man by six o'clock.

" But you aren't going bathing, Mary," he expostulated, for Mary had on her bathing drawers and her blue bow.

" Red, white and blue," said Mary pointing. " I'm jubileeing to-day."

" You are ! " said the Owl Man. " But most people go jubileeing in rosettes and if you wear those drawers I shan't get you a rosette. Just as you like, of course, but it must be the drawers or the rosette—not both."

" What kind of a rosette ? " enquired Mary, cautiously.

" Large and frilly, made of silk," said the Owl Man. " Perhaps a flag, too."

" I unchoose my bathing drawers," said Mary.

Mark joined them after breakfast and they set out for their stand in the Green Park, looking very gay with their rosettes and Jubilee expressions.

" Do I say ' Hurray ' or ' Hurrah ' to the King ? " asked Mary, anxiously.

" Now, that's a very serious question to settle," said the Owl Man. " We don't want to go and spoil the King's whole day by saying the wrong thing. What do you think, Mark ? "

But Mark was in explosions of laughter and was no good at all.

" I'll say both," decided Mary. " What are their names ? Just King and Queen ? "

" King George and Queen Mary," said Mark.

" *Mary !* Oh dear," and Mary gave a huge sigh. " Aren't I a lucky bear ? "

" Why ? " asked Mark.

" Having a Queen for my twin, of course," said Mary. " Now I've got two twins."

" Now," said the Owl Man, as they got out of their taxi at Hyde Park Corner, " hang on to me, and if either of you get lost, ask for Stand Twenty-Two."

The crowd was immense and Mary was small and halfway across the road she got swept away from the others.

For a moment they tried to find her and called her name but the jamb was terrific and finally the Owl Man said it was quite hopeless—they'd better go to the stand and wait ; Mary knew what to do and she had a lot of sense. All the same, he looked more and more anxious as the moments passed and no Mary appeared and, when the streets were cleared from traffic and

The seven policemen stood around at the bottom

the distant sound of music told of the arrival of the troops to line the route, he felt quite frantic.

"I'd go and look for her but you might as well look for a needle in a hay-stack," he said, "I've a better chance of spotting her from here. I must just wait."

He didn't have to wait long. Round the corner of Constitution Hill in close formation swung the Guards, looking in their smart red coats as if someone had just cut the string and let them out of their box. Cheers greeted their progress but suddenly there was a difference in the cheering—a kind of a shout and a whoop which made everybody crane their heads to look at the cause.

The cause was Mary, marching a couple of yards in front of the band with a paw held stiffly to attention.

"Jehoshaphat!" murmured the Owl Man, too paralysed to move.

But someone else moved. A large policeman followed by six others started to run towards her. Seeing them, Mary took sudden fright, sped across the open space towards an island, and in a moment she had swarmed to the top of the lamp-post. The seven policemen stood around the bottom and looked up at her, shaking their fists, while Mary, safe, and therefore quite unconcerned, looked over their heads and enjoyed a better view of the crowds and decorations than anyone else.

"They'll never get her to come down," said the Owl Man, who still seemed to be rooted to the spot and unable to move.

"Hadn't you better go?" suggested Mark and then, "Hallo, here comes the fire-engine, how thrilling!"

Sure enough, up Piccadilly came thundering an engine with bell clanging and great folded red ladders. Everyone began to look about for the fire when, to their amazement, the engine drew up under Mary's lamp-post and a great roar went up as the crowd realised it had come to rescue her. To an accompaniment of shouts and hoots the ladder was unfolded to its full length and a shy and rather unwilling fireman started to climb up towards Mary.

It took a good ten minutes to persuade her to come down and during that ten minutes the Owl Man fought and pushed his way through the crowd and arrived underneath the lamppost just as Mary reached the bottom. At first the seven policemen wanted to arrest her but the Owl Man pointed out that she had done no harm and, being a foreign bear, she could hardly be expected to know lamp-post climbing was forbidden —especially at Jubilees. As it was getting very late, the policemen let her go and the Owl Man, amid friendly jeers from the crowd, got her back to the stand just as the Procession was due.

" Phew ! " he said sitting down and mopping his forehead with his handkerchief.

" That was a pretty near shave," said a man sitting on Mary's other side. She turned and looked at him. He had the kind of face she liked.

" Did you see me marching ? " she enquired pleasantly.

" I did," said the man, " and I liked the way you climbed that lamp-post, too."

" The policemen didn't," said Mary.

" No, they wouldn't be likely to," said the man. " They never like anything unusual, I've noticed."

Mary beamed. " I can't help being unusual sometimes because, you see, I am an unusual first-class bear with a white rosette and a gold medal with a picture of myself on it, and, and—"

" Oh, shut up, Mary," growled the Owl Man who was still too hot to bear Mary's list.

" And," finished Mary, " I do like Jubilees."

" Well, you'd better enjoy this one as much as you can," said the Owl Man, " because it'll be your last."

" Why ? " asked Mary, but the Owl Man never answered as just then the Procession began.

Because of their being in the back row and the shortness of Mary's legs she couldn't see, so the two men lifted her up on to the bar behind them and there, with a paw on each of their shoulders to steady her, she had an excellent view. She lurched rather dangerously as the two little Princesses passed, as it is difficult to wave and balance at the same time.

" Steady there, Mary," warned the Owl Man. " Here comes the Prince of Wales."

" Why has he got a fur head ? " enquired Mary, between her cheers. But the answer was drowned in the growing roar of sound which told them that the great moment had come and along came the exciting trotting Horse Guards and behind them, most exciting of all, the King and Queen.

" Hurrah, King ! Hurray, King ! " yelled Mary. " Hurrah, Queen-twin ! " and waving wildly with both paws, she lost her balance and dived head foremost into the people two rows ahead. There she remained till the King and Queen passed out of sight, her head wedged and two furry legs kicking frantically. The Owl Man climbed over the row between and, catching her by one leg, gave a pull.

" Ow," said Mary and " Really ! " said the people, who, now that the Procession had gone, had time to be annoyed at being dived into by a strange bear. The lamp-post episode

had been amusing but when it came to being dived into—
well, there were some things one didn't do at Processions.

"I'm terribly sorry," apologised the harassed Owl Man.
"She over-balanced."

"I over-hurrahed myself off the bar," explained Mary,
rubbing her head ruefully and looking a bit glum.

Back in their own row her new friend looked at her with
rather a twinkle.

"Well," he said, "lots of people got terribly excited but I
don't believe anyone else actually stood on their heads while
the King and Queen passed.   Have some chocolate to refresh
you."

"Thank you," said Mary.   What a particularly nice man
this was!   "I like chocolate—it's one of my favourite eats."

"She's a friendly cub," said the man to the Owl Man.

"I like being friendly," said Mary, finishing his last slab
of chocolate.   "I like lots of things."

"Do you, now?   What kind of things?"

"Well, meringues and Kings and winning things and labels
and twins and school colours and letters and—and—"

"Talking," put in the Owl Man.

The other man laughed and got up.   "Well, I must be

getting along," he said. "But, look here, you write to me and tell me the rest, will you?"

"But you couldn't read my writing," said Mary. "it's very special."

"I bet I could," said the man. "Just you try me. Here's my address," and he scribbled on a scrap of paper and gave it to Mary and waving his hand, went off.

"Come on, Mary," said the Owl Man, "we must go, too."

"But what a little address," said Mary. "Look!"

The Owl Man looked. "Hallo!" he said. "Hallo!" For on the card was written, *Mac. B.B.C.*

"Do you know who you've been talking to, Mary?"

"Who?" asked Mary.

"Why your friend Uncle Mac."

"Him what's on the wire-phone?" asked Mary excitedly.

"None other," said the Owl Man, while Mark sighed and said, "Mary *does* have luck, doesn't she?"

CHAPTER FOURTEEN

MARY GOES TO THE B.B.C.

MARY did not forget to write her letter to Uncle Mac. She sent him quite a long list of things she liked that she hadn't had time to tell him about at the Jubilee, ending with, " I like all the voices what talk but specially yours because now I know what kind of face it lives in. I like it too, when it's the *Teddy Bears' Picnic* because that's about me and I like things about me."

Next day a letter arrived addressed to Miss Mary Plain, G.M.

" What's the G.M. for ? " asked Mary.

" I can't think," said the Owl Man. " Gracious me, or Good Mary—it might be anything. Look inside."

Inside was written,

Dear Miss Plain,

Thank you for your letter. I am so glad you enjoy the Children's Hour. I wonder if you would come along on Friday evening and give the children a little talk? It would be a delightful addition to our programme and I am sure you would do it charmingly.

Yours sincerely,

Uncle Mac.

Mary looked up with her eyes shining. "Isn't he kind?" she said.

"Almost too kind, I think," said the Owl Man, who often wished Mary was a less public character.

All the same he got home on Friday in good time to give her a good brushing and get her ready for her visit.

They went in a taxi. The driver politely opened the door.

"I'm going to the A.B.C.," Mary told him, "to give a talk."

"Really!" said the man, wondering if it was a lecture on penny buns.

"To the B.B.C." corrected the Owl Man, as he got in after her.

All the way in the taxi Mary had guesses about what G.M. meant. The inside of the B.B.C. was rather like a hospital and Mary clung to the Owl Man's hand. "I haven't got measles again," she said uneasily, "I don't prickle anywhere."

"Don't be a silly little goose," said the Owl Man.

Uncle Mac was waiting for them in the studio. He held a small girl by the hand who kept hopping up and down.

"What's the G.M.?" asked Mary at once.

" Why, Gold Medallist, of course," said Uncle Mac surprised. " I naturally thought you would wish to have your full title on your letters."

" Oh yes, I always do," said Mary hastily, while the Owl Man cleared his throat in the background.

" Does she ever stop ? " asked Mary, pointing at the little girl.

" Stop what ? "

" Hopping. Does she just hop because she feels hoppy ? "

" Well, you see, it is rather exciting to meet a bear for the first time."

" Especially an unusual one," said Mary, gravely.

" Exactly. Now, Judith, you stop hopping and shake hands with Miss Plain." So Judith stopped for just long enough to say how do you do.

"I expect you have often heard Elisabeth and Barbara talk," went on Uncle Mac, "and here they are."

"It's very exciting to meet voices," said Mary.

"It's very exciting for us to meet ears," said Elisabeth.

"Ears?" said Mary. "How do you mean, ears?"

"Well, if we're the voices that talk, you're the ears that listen, do you see?"

"Yes," said Mary, who didn't.

Uncle Mac clapped his hands. "Now, when that light there goes on, everybody must stop talking," he said.

The light went on and Uncle Mac and Elisabeth and Barbara all stepped up to the microphone.

"Good evening, children," said Uncle Mac.

"Good evening, children," said Elisabeth.

"Good evening, children," said Barbara.

"There's a—" said Mary.

"Ssh!" said everybody—at Mary.

"Now, this evening, children," said Uncle Mac, "we are starting our programme with a—"

"I say, there's a—" began Mary again, and "Ssh!" said everybody very sternly.

"With a few songs which have been especially written for the Children's Hour. The first is called—"

"There's a—" began Mary.

"*Bluebell growing in my garden*!" finished Uncle Mac neatly. "Now, Miss Black, if you will begin!" He crossed to where Mary was sitting and shook his head at her.

"Look here," he whispered, "you mustn't talk in here, you know."

"I only wanted to tell them there's a bear in the studio

tonight," said Mary, reproachfully. " Why didn't you let me ? "

" Because it wasn't the right moment," answered Uncle Mac. " All speakers have to be introduced properly."

" Am I one then ? "

" One what ? "

" One squeaker ?"

" *Speaker*, I said."

" So did I " lied Mary quickly.

" Of course you are," said Uncle Mac.

" Is it an important thing to be ? " asked Mary next in a hoarse whisper.

" Very," said Uncle Mac.

And because importance was one of her favourite things and she loved introductions, when she was the one that was being introduced, Mary said no more.

" I say," whispered Uncle Mac after a few moments," have you thought of what you are going to say yet ? "

" Not yet," said Mary. " I've been too busy. I can't listen and think all together."

" Well, I'll leave you to think quietly," said Uncle Mac, " because in ten minutes it will be time for you to begin."

During those ten minutes Barbara read a rather thrilling story about a porcupine and Mary listened enthralled and never remembered about the thinking till she saw Uncle Mac coming towards her again. Then she got suddenly frightened. What was she going to say ? She didn't want to talk into the wire-phone. She'd rather stay safely with the Owl Man. Why had she left the nice safe pits ! She tugged at the Owl

Man's arm. "Do you think the twins are happy without me?" she asked.

The Owl Man sprang to the rescue. "You bet they are!" he said. "Think how jealous they'll be when they hear you've been broadcasting. Why! Friska would give her eyes to have such an exciting chance."

Friska's eyes did the trick. Mary consented to be helped up on to a tall chair opposite the microphone while Uncle Mac, remembering her Jubilee dive, put his arm as far round her middle as it would go.

And this is what the children at the other end heard.*

U. Mac. : "Now, children, our next item is to be a surprise talk from a surprise visitor—"

Mary : ("S'visitor.")

U. Mac. : "S'visitor. (Sorry). She has come from the bear-pits at Berne and I am sure what she is going to say will interest you very much."

Mary : ("Yes—I'll tell them lots of exciting things.")

U. Mac. : ("What about?")

Mary : ("About me and Mary and Mary Plain—all of us. What's the Owl Man making that funny noise in his throat for? Has he got a cold?")

U. Mac. : ("No, he's all right.) Now, children, I want to introduce Miss Mary Plain."

Mary : ("Have they guessed I'm a bear?")

U. Mac. : ("I expect so, because of the address.")

Mary : ("'Bear-pits' is a very beary address, isn't it?")

U. Mac. : ("It is.) Now, Miss Mary Plain."

Mary : ("Do I begin now?")

* All conversation in brackets to be spoken in a loud whisper.

U. Mac. : ("Please.")

Mary : ("Introduce me again, please, I wasn't quite ready.")

U. Mac. : "Miss—Mary—Plain."

Mary : "An unusual first-class bear from the bear-pits at Berne, with a white rosette and a gold medal with a picture of me on it. (They'll know now, won't they?)"

U. Mac. : ("They will.) Tell me, Miss Plain, do you ever feel homesick at all?"

Mary : "Pit-sick, do you mean?"

U. Mac. : "I suppose I do."

Mary : "No, but I sometimes feel twin-sick because of playing with them. But I don't ever feel even a tiny bit Friska-sick."

U. Mac. : "And who is Friska?"

Mary : "She's my aunt—a very aunty aunt what gives us lessons."

U. Mac. : "I see—and what other bears are there in the pits?"

Mary : "Well, there's Bunch. He sits on the tree and catches the biggest carrots—he's a very greedy kind of bear, is Bunch. (I think the Owl Man has got a cold. Bet I put a hot sandbag on him to-night?")

U. Mac. : ("Don't you worry about him, he's quite all right.) And is that all the bears there are?"

Mary : "Oh, no, there's Forget-me-not and Plum, only they're too little to matter and there's Big Wool; she's very strict and un-playey, and there used to be Harrods."

U. Mac. : "Where is Harrods now?"

Mary : "She's gone to live with St. Bruin because he wanted her. We didn't."

U. Mac. : "Didn't you like her?"

Mary : " No, she was very cross and both her eyes looked at her nose. And then, of course there's Alpha and Lady Grizzle."

U. Mac. : " Who are they ? "

Mary : " They're very old and special and when we go and svisit them we say a pome. Shall I say it now ? "

U. Mac. : " Please."

Mary : " *Many happy years we wish to you*
May carrots and dried figs your pit-floor strew,
We hope that happiness will with you stay,
Till we all meet on next St. Bruin's Day.

By Friska."

U. Mac. : " Thank you very much. It's a beautiful poem. And now, Miss Plain, I am afraid your time is up."

Mary : " Oh, but I haven't begun yet."

U. Mac. : "I'm awfully sorry. You must come again one day soon and then—"

Mary : " Then I'll be able to tell them some things about me next time, about my being unusual and first-class and having a white rose—"

U. Mac. : " Quite. Now, children, I am sure we are all most grateful to Miss Plain for coming and as this is her first visit—"

Mary : (" Svisit.")

U. Mac. : " Svisit (Sorry), to the B.B.C. let's all give her a real good send off. We here in the Studio are all joining hands in a circle and Miss Plain is standing on a chair in the middle and I believe she's wondering what we're going to sing. Now, you can't join in our circle, children, but

you can join in the song, wherever you are, so altogether—"
And all over England, all the children sang as loud as they
could,

> *For she's a jolly good fellow*
> *For she's a jolly good fellow*
> *For she's a jolly good fellow*
> *And so say all of us !*
> *And so say all of us,*
> *And so say all of us !*
> *For she's a jolly good fellow*
> *And so say all of us !*

Elisabeth : " Good-night, children."
Barbara : " Good-night, children."
Uncle Mac. : " Good-night, children."
Mary : " Good-night, children.   (That's me—Mary Plain ! ")